The Australian Pen Pal

By Michelle Linn-Gust

CHELLEHEAD
WORKS

ISBN# 978-0-9723318-6-9
Library of Congress Control Number: 2011909292

Chellehead Works
info@chelleheadworks.com
505-266-3134 (voice)
Albuquerque, New Mexico

Printed in the United States of America
First Edition June 2011

Designed by Megan Herndon

For Debbie,

The real Australian pen pal

Table of Contents

Chapter 1

Rachel Monroe slid into her seat on the airplane and settled in for the flight to Los Angeles from Kansas. When the plane took off down the runway, she watched the green Kansas grass wave in the open wind and it reminded her of how she felt; just going with the flow where the wind was taking her. She wasn't totally sure what this trip would mean to her life but something told her that it wouldn't be the same when she returned home in four weeks.

And when her second flight left Los Angeles in the darkness hours later, only the lit Pacific Coast visible behind her when she looked back, she thought of everything she was leaving behind for thirty days. She'd been given an opportunity and she chose to seize it. Now she'd see where it took her while home could wait.

During the flight, Rachel reached into her bag under the seat in front of her and pulled out several letters and clippings held together by a rubber band. These weren't the only ones she had but they were the one she chose to take with her. The cassette tapes would have been too bulky and the pink t-shirt with the name "Australia" straight across it and a Koala hanging onto one of the letters didn't fit anymore. The size of the fourteen-year-old Rachel who had worn it didn't exist anymore.

They had been in a box with her junior high and high school yearbooks. She hadn't kept much from her life, mostly because her mother kept making her take boxes each time she'd visit. Finally, before their last move, Tom put them in a stack in the middle of their family room and told her that he wasn't moving them. She had to go through them first.

"You never seem anxious to take them when we visit your mom," he reminded her, "so surely you don't want the things in them."

But Tom, observant architect that he was, at least chose a time when she wasn't busy. He waited until school let out for the spring semester.

"No excuses," he had added, wagging a finger at Rachel. Then he'd fold his arms as he stood in front of her. As he stared at her, she would think about something in that chin of his that she loved. And that's what made her attack the contents as much as she would rather have been digging in her garden.

1

She'd eliminated two of the six boxes easily. The rest he would put in the attic of the new house. Rachel hated to go up there to find everything she needed before her trip. She knew that next to the boxes of her childhood, the history that she now realized some people might find interesting, were the boxes of what was left of Tom's life. And those had been much more painful to let go of. It had taken her almost a year to clean out his underwear drawer.

"Underwear!" she had exclaimed to her friends. "Of all the lame things I couldn't let go of."

Rachel wasn't sure if she thought it was because he might be coming back and need them. It didn't make sense because she had watched the cancer ravage his body, age him, and leave him so that she didn't recognize him in the end. Except for the chin.

It all had forced her to change. She leaned her head against the window, the shade now pulled down per the flight attendant's instructions, and hoped he was with her in some way. As much as Rachel missed Tom, she had come to terms with that part of her life ending a long time ago. It had surfaced in her first novel, *Runaway Heart*, and the career as a writer that she'd always dreamed of. She knew Tom had orchestrated it. That gave her the comfort she needed to plug away.

The man beside her was nice, she thought, when she decided to get up in the middle of the flight to use the lavatory. He was Asian. She was grateful that no one was in the seat between them, allowing more space to spread out. Rachel couldn't get interested in reading anything as the flight progressed. Something put her in a reflective mood and she wished she could raise the window shade, if only to see the darkness of the Pacific Ocean below, but she feared the wrath of the flight attendant who already gave her grief about asking for a blanket.

"Since when do we have to beg for blankets on an international flight?" she wondered out loud to the Asian man after the woman had passed by.

"Cutbacks," the man said, pretending he had scissors in his hand.

Rachel curled up underneath the blanket with the small pillow under her head and turned on her headphones. While she was hoping for sleep, she was realistic to know that she probably was going to do more thinking instead.

And remembering.

She wished that Tom was making this trip with her. She couldn't believe how much her life had changed since he died. She remembered the day they met at the grocery store. He had been "fondling" the lemons as she later told everyone. Rachel almost had run into Tom with her cart. She was looking for the limes and didn't see the man in front of the lemons which were next to the limes.

They struck up a conversation first about citrus and then about key lime pie, something she was making that weekend for a party at her house. That's when he told her he was going to a barbecue that weekend and maybe she would bring the pie with her?

Rachel had laughed since she already had plans for the pie but offered to make another. They talked on the phone for several hours over the next few days. She couldn't believe when he showed up at her doorstep and wasn't planning to take her anywhere. In his arms he held several bags of groceries.

"I thought we were going to a barbecue?" she had questioned him, when he asked to be led to her kitchen.

He put the bags down and wiped his hand across his sweaty shaved head. Kansas summer humidity made everyone sweat but Tom's shaved head always looked shiny when it happened. Their friends constantly joked about his bowling ball head.

"Well, we were, but I decided after talking to you on the phone the last few days that I'd rather spend the evening with you and continue our conversations." He proceeded to make himself at home in her townhouse kitchen and cook dinner on her grill. They capped it off with key lime pie.

Rachel smiled at the memory. She knew Tom was someone special then. He didn't waste time with her. He acted like there was no time to waste in life. They were married in two years. And their first date became a scene in her third novel, I See You.

Only her closest friends and family knew how many times Tom appeared in her works. But now she was done using facets of Tom as a character. She saw writing about him as a way to help her cope with her loss, but she thought in some way she used it to help her let go of the daydreams she had about the rest of the life they would never have. After all, I See You, was about the length of a marriage and all it entailed. And how it all changed and endured in that time. She never admitted what she wrote was based on fact. She simply told every-

3

one that she used her own experience and that of everyone in her life as a basis for her writing.

The plane hit some turbulence and she remembered telling Tom about Jenny for the first time.

"It's been with me for so long," she tried to explain, knowing that somehow he understood. "I don't know what happened but I need to figure it out."

"You'll get to Australia," he had said. "There's no doubt about that."

But somewhere between when she told him about that dream, and her getting on the plane to Australia, she had let it go. Years went by. The dream had died. Or so she thought. Jenny Phillips didn't seem so important. Maybe because she was caught up in the present. Tom was her life as were her students at the university. Those were the things that made her tick, not the things that she thought at one time in her life might make her tick as an adult.

And the day when she and Tom were lying together on the couch, after the cancer had taken its toll on him physically, he asked her what her future plans were.

"Oh, please don't ask me that," she had cried. "How can you ask me? You won't be here, you know. I can't think that far in advance."

No matter how much she protested, he begged, "Please just answer the question."

"The truth is," she said, trying not to cry, "I don't know. I can't even think past dinner tonight and I haven't even thought about that because I haven't asked you what you want."

He grabbed her as tightly as he could and she felt him whisper into her ear. "Here's the deal," he said. "I want you to go back and think about every goal and dream you've ever had that you haven't accomplished yet. I know there are some on your list. I believe there are some you've forgotten." He had to stop and catch his breath. She watched his hands, looking like they belonged to an old man rather than the middle-aged man that Tom was.

By now Rachel couldn't stop crying. He was asking her to go on, to think about the future. But that was a scary place to go since Tom had been in her life for ten years. She'd gotten used to, no comfortable, with sharing it with him.

She knew she'd even miss the annoying things about him, like when he chased her around the house to kiss her with his morning breath, something she tried to allow but couldn't bring herself to accept . How much time she had wasted asking him to brush his teeth first in the morning. That was sacred time they couldn't get back now.

"I want you to go out and accomplish them. And if it includes marrying a man with a head full of curly hair, do that, too," he said. He kissed a spot where her forehead met her scalp. "You have a full life ahead of you. You've given up a lot of time to be with me and take care of me while I'm dying. I just want to know that in return, you'll do everything you've ever set out to do."

Rachel tried to promise. She said it through her tears although on that late morning she wasn't sure if she could really do it.

After Tom died, it would take her some time to focus again. He died in the spring, March 5th, to be exact, Her sabbatical from the university wasn't up until August. That meant she had until then to grieve and figure out what was next. She wasn't down for long.

She missed Tom, there was no doubt about that, but she had promised she would honor him and that life would continue after his death. She allowed herself time to be sad, but one day something inside her began to stir when she woke up.

No longer was she looking next to her each morning to see if he was still sleeping. She didn't look for him to see if he was waiting for her to wake up for some morning sex. Instead, she woke up looking out the window at the day that had started out there. Summer was in bloom by then and the trees were filled with green leaves, shading the lawn and her garden in the back yard. The morning was fresh, ready to be tackled. It looked different than it had recently and that meant it was time for her to see what she might do with it.

Rachel didn't start with a list of her goals and dreams. Instead, she took her morning walk and then sat in the kitchen with her coffee and a frozen waffle topped with strawberries and syrup. The garden needed planting. But so did Rachel. She pulled her blonde hair up on top of her head and tied it there. Then she found a blank notebook and opened it on the table in front of her and started writing with the bank pen she had picked up the other day.

That hadn't been enough though. After two pages of notes, she realized she needed to sit at the computer. There was too much there, her thoughts were going too fast so she poured it all out to her laptop.

And slowly she formed and shaped it, just as she thought she would do if some-one handed her a block of clay, into a story. Each day on her walk, she thought about what she needed to add next, what holes she needed to fill. Sometimes she figured out characteristics and themes when she was out surveying the neighborhood. They came easily when she was walking. It was almost as if Tom was speaking to her through her walks and that flowed through to her writing. He knew how important this dream had been to her at one time.

"You better make the bestseller list," he had teased her each New Year's Day when they reflected on the last year and looked forward to what they were go-ing to do in the new year. And in each passing year, Rachel's dream of writing fiction seemed to slip away.

Life events had done that. The dream had been pushed away, just like papers on a table that were in the way at dinnertime, leaving Rachel some time ago to wonder why she was hanging on to it. She would sigh as she looked at the one item she kept putting on her list each year but didn't accomplish.

That same day on the couch, Tom reminded her of that dream. "Don't forget the writing dream. Spend a little less time grading your students' papers and a little more time writing for you. The candle is still flickering."

But as she wrote, it wasn't that she didn't miss Tom. She still thought about him. Sometimes she wanted to share things with him. And she did anyway, talking to him as if he was there. But she also knew that she finally admitted there had been a resentful side to her at one time. Taking care of him had been a lot of work. She had to reconcile that in her life her students were going on without her that year.

Now, though, she was free. And she could write all night long if she needed to. Just as Tom really wanted to her to do, even when he was sick, but she had refused. She thought she needed to be with him every second of the day when possible because their days, their hours, and their minutes together were num-bered.

"But yours are, too," he had laughed one evening. "You just appear to have more of them than I do." Rachel curled up closer to him instead of opening the laptop and starting to write.

On a Wednesday morning that summer after Tom died, she called the four clos-est friends she could count on to meet her at her house on a Friday night. She would make burritos and margaritas, what they all loved to come to Rachel and Tom's house for, and hand them each a copy of the manuscript.

"I need to know it works," she said to them. Chris and Stephanie burst into tears as they flipped through it.

"How did you ever find the strength to do this?" they asked almost in unison. Kara and Tanya looked a little stunned.

Rachel poured herself a margarita and sat down with her friends. "Tom made me promise to accomplish all the goals I set and never did. So here's the first one."

"This isn't exactly a small one," Tanya reminded her, putting down the reading glasses she had recently begun to wear.

She found an agent several months later and *Runaway Heart* was published the next year. When people couldn't believe she'd made it happen that fast, she knew that wasn't true. It had been a long time coming. And life hadn't been the same since. Each time Rachel saw a copy at a bookstore or in someone's hand, she closed her eyes and thanked Tom for helping her make that dream come true.

*****

Watching the baggage carousel was not one of Rachel's favorite things to do. It drove her crazy to watch people cram their way in front of her as if they knew for sure that their luggage would come out before hers. And she always felt anxiety about going through customs. She knew one day her bag would get searched. It had been a lot of work to pack it just right, to meet the airline's weight limit, to include everything she needed. And someone was going to mess that up. It also didn't sound like much of a welcome into any country. Or a welcome home to the United States. Rachel thought they should take all the welcome signs down and place them outside customs.

When her two bags finally made their way toward her, she grabbed them and wondered what Australia was really like. Airports appeared the same no matter where she was, she always thought. The baggage carousels were long and the ceilings low. Maybe that was to help people acclimate by making them the same, she wondered, dragging her bags, her passport, and declaration form to the security man who directed her to the left. Sometimes the language changed. So did the cell phone carriers advertised. Yet, ultimately, they were all the same.

After sending her bags through an x-ray machine, Rachel tried to reach for them all and organize herself for the trip outside to find a taxi to the hotel.

"You should get a trolley," the man with surgical gloves working for the Australian government suggested.

Rachel could only smile. She had no clue what he had said. And later when she realized that he had suggested a trolley, she only could think of the buses that ran in certain places. Not 'baggage carts' as they were called in the United States.

The biggest surprise would be everything on the wrong side of the road but for left-hander Rachel it actually gave her a sense of relief to be somewhere in the world where they appreciated the ways of the left handed. She almost felt at home each time she went somewhere where people drove on the left, walked on the left, and thought on the left.

This was the place she had longed to visit most of her life, not really ever understanding why. Jenny Phillips certainly helped facilitate it but it really had started long before she came into Rachel's life. Still, something drew her there and when she sat in the taxi as the driver maneuvered his way through traffic, she felt a sense of "Oh, I came home."

Chapter 2

The hotel sat near Ruscutter's Bay. Not that it meant much to Rachel since she had no idea where in Sydney she was. She looked out her window at the boats in the water and the green park between the hotel and the water where a group of men played soccer. This must be life in Sydney, she thought, opening her laptop and pulling her dress out of her luggage. She jumped into the shower to help herself feel normal again once she scrubbed off the travel, then sat down at her laptop, the screen blank in front of her.

Rachel thought there were three distinct segments to her trip: first the work part, then the beach part, and in between she had another manuscript to write. That was her usual summer task. They were aiming for novel number five. She put the laptop down and popped her shoes on instead. It could wait.

I have almost four weeks to do it, she thought, brushing her now dried hair.

Rachel walked around the hotel, opting to scope out the rooftop swimming pool first. No one was there and she relaxed on a lounge chair someone had pulled over to the glass railing allowing a person to lay down and still see the boats moored in the bay. While it was windy, the sun was warm. She wondered if it was cool or warm for a typical fall day. At home in the fall, campus would be crawling with students as the leaves began to turn color. Reality was that in the northern hemisphere they were all working at their summer jobs.

A group of men chased a ball on the lush field below. In another area of the park, several dogs ran around while their owners stood by, cups of coffee in their hands, and watched. She was exhausted but it was morning and she knew the worst mistake she could make was to go to bed now. She had to find some way to keep herself awake most of the day.

Although breakfast had ended in the restaurant, the woman at the desk told Rachel on the phone that they were open. As Rachel sat down in the airy room, she combed the menu looking for something warm that didn't scream "Airline food!" on it. A bowl of soup sounded good, she thought, summoning the waiter.

While she waited for her meal, Rachel used the time to think about the new manuscript. She had some idea of the characters and some inkling of what would happen. The main character's name was Melinda. But something was different this time. For four novels, she had drawn on the strength of Tom and her loss to help her mold the story. But this time she felt that she had to get the strength from somewhere else.

Where? She wondered.

Tom had been dead five years and she had used him constantly to help her with the stories. Lately the answer always came back as, "No, it's time. You didn't really need me before. I just facilitated it for you. Now you need to find the strength elsewhere." Rachel knew he was right.

What would the conflict be this time? Usually that was the easy part and then she built the characters around that. It felt backward to have her characters and not really know what would be the internal struggle.

She didn't tell Marian, her editor, what she was up against. No one knew. They just knew she had a deadline in August to deliver another manuscript. And Rachel thought she would make it. As the fish chowder was delivered, she wasn't worried yet. Four weeks in Australia had to cure it.

Maybe an afternoon by the pool with a book, she thought, not anxious to go back to her room and hide in the little box. She didn't feel alive enough yet to wander the city.

"Don't!" her friends had warned, concerned for her safety. "We know how lost you get on a good day! Stay close to the hotel until you feel somewhat normal."

At least Rachel knew she could count on them for solid advice. They knew her better than anyone else now that Tom was gone and the rest of her family was living in Michigan.

She spent the afternoon at the pool until the clouds rolled in. She ordered a pizza that night and found herself tucked into bed by 7:00 pm. That was okay. She had to work at 8:00 am.

Chapter 3

They said she was becoming a star in Australia. As Rachel kept her eyes closed for the makeup application at the television studio, she wondered what that meant. She knew she had a following in the U.S. but the publicist at the publisher had insisted that something had happened in Australia. It involved the woman they called "the Australian Oprah."

"Her name is Miranda Connor and she apparently picked up your book one day and read it while 'on holiday' as they say," Jill had said. "She mentioned it on air and sales went through the roof. They didn't even have enough copies in the country."

So now Rachel was in Australia to appear on Miranda's show and do several book signings along the eastern coast. And for her vacation.

"But don't forget you have another book due before you return to teaching in the fall," Marian the editor reminded her one last time before Rachel left.

The semester was over, the papers were graded. And the office door was locked behind her. Rachel had the summer to herself.

Almost.

"You'll go next door to the hairdresser," the woman said, taking the protective cape off Rachel and pointing to the door. The woman there blew dry any curl out of Rachel's long blonde hair. She thought her hair was stiffer than a board when she was done. It wasn't going anywhere even if there were wind gusts on the set. She wondered if they had something planned she didn't know about.

By the time Rachel reached the set, she had been at the studio two hours, passing the rest of her time in the green room. The festive crew miked Rachel and made jokes with Miranda who sat in her chair next to the couch where they would lead Rachel to sit.

Rachel worried as she looked down at her feet though. It was fall in Australia and the previous guests wore their long boots. She wore her black slides. This wasn't good. She tried not to be self conscious. It was spring at home, she would tell them. Rachel had put her boots away for the winter a long time ago and she didn't have room for them in the luggage anyway.

But when she looked over at Miranda's feet, Miranda had on pumps. Rachel sighed. Crisis adverted. She didn't want everyone to remember her as the author on television who wore slides while everyone wore boots.

"Oh, I am so happy to meet you," Miranda said, when Rachel was on the carpeted area. She got up and took Rachel's hand. The possible boot debacle was quickly forgotten.

"Well, I guess you're the person I owe my visit to," Rachel laughed.

"*Summer Bay* was the best book I've ever read," Miranda sighed happily. "The characters, the feeling. You made me feel like I was there."

When the commercials ended and the cameras focused on the two of them talking in Miranda's so-called living room, nothing changed. Miranda wanted to know all about the characters and the setting. How did Rachel come up with the idea for the story? What was next?

Rachel hoped her cringe didn't show when Miranda asked about the future. That was a contention between her and her editor right now. Rachel had the summer to write another book. She had been clear with them that it would wait until the semester was over and the college students had gone home, like every other book she had written in the summer. The students were still her priority as long as she was employed by the university.

But she had something even larger to admit to herself. What was the struggle going to be?

"Oh, I've got something up my sleeve," Rachel said with a sly smile. "But I don't want to give too much away." She knew it was the easy way to get out of the question. No one would question her keeping the story a secret. "It takes away from the story telling if I start spouting off too much before it's written," she added.

When the interview ended and Rachel was in her cab cruising through the city back to the hotel, she wondered how many people saw it. If Miranda was as popular as everyone indicated, then the books would fly off the stacks that evening at the store in Sydney. Even Miranda had Rachel sign her own dog-eared copy.

Most importantly though, had Jenny seen it? Would she ever know?

Rachel could still remember when she and Jenny Phillips became pen pals. When she was fourteen, someone had told her about an organization that could put her in touch with other people her age. A pen pal. Since it was long before the Internet, it was all done via snail mail. Rachel thought it cost her seventy-five cents per name. She selected four countries: Australia, Sweden, Mexico, and Germany. She came from German descent, that was easy. She was taking Spanish in the fall and thought maybe she could use what she learned on her pen pal. She thought Sweden was cool; they had those great cookies with the nuts and the powdered sugar. But it was Australia that was most important.

And there was no way that Rachel could understand it. Her obsession with Australia began at a very young age when watching an episode of the television show "The Love Boat." Her best friend Lindsay and she used to play "Love Boat" (they never said it with "The"), something their mothers often laughed about. The two girls sailed off to far away places and used the lawn chairs in their backyards as deck chairs and their homes' wooden decks to portray one of the pool decks on the ship. They knew nothing about actual cruise ships, only what they saw on television every Saturday night right before "Fantasy Island."

They made themselves Captain Stubing's daughters, much like Vickie, and had what they thought were romances with men who varied by the day. Finally, the plastic pool that Lindsey had at her house for her younger brother and sister usually took the place of a much larger pool.

An episode of "The Love Boat" introduced Rachel to Australia. Cruise Director Julie was getting married and the whole crew took a trip Down Under since her husband-to-be was Australian. While Rachel hadn't seen the episode since she was young, it stuck with her. She wanted to go to Australia even though Julie ended up not getting married and sailing away with her friends back to their usual route along the coast of Mexico.

The other pen pals didn't pan out. Rachel was convinced her bad Spanish confused the Mexican girl, the German boy never wrote back, and she and the Swedish girl only wrote a few times.

It was the summer before ninth grade when Jenny Phillips wrote back. Suddenly she was more than just a name on a computer-generated piece of paper. She was a girl the same age as Rachel but in another country. Another hemisphere even.

Rachel's mom was taking Rachel to get a perm that afternoon. Rachel was so excited to have a piece a mail. And to make her long straight blonde hair go curly.

The hairdresser asked her about school and what she would be doing that summer but all Rachel wanted to think about was going home and writing Jenny back. It wasn't a long letter but long enough to give Rachel some general details about Jenny. She lived in Coolum Beach in Queensland and she had two sisters. Her birthday was in January. And she looked forward to coming to America one day.

Rachel pulled out the world atlas in the family room bookcase to see exactly where Jenny lived. As she pondered it over the kitchen table, her mother came from the sink where she had been cleaning up from their spaghetti dinner. "Maybe one day you'll get there," Connie Ramsay said.

"I hope so," Rachel told her, closing the atlas, but keeping her fingers in place on the page as if when she closed her eyes, they would guide her wish to coming true.

It didn't take Rachel long to pop out a four-page letter back to her new friend. She told her all about the music she liked, her favorite television shows, how she was going to be a writer some day, and that she was playing tennis for her high school that fall. She enclosed a photo and rode her bike to downtown Sycamore Springs, to the small post office where she stood in line with her coins to pay for the stamp to send the letter off to Jenny.

And then she waited.

That summer was a pivotal one for Rachel's life. She was going into high school and had made the decision to play competitive tennis that fall. While she'd been playing quite a bit since she was in fourth grade, it would be her first encounter with playing on a team. Lindsey had already decided to join the swim team but they were still just as good friends, even though they'd long given up playing "Love Boat."

It was that summer that Rachel's brother Brandon took both Rachel and Lindsey to see U2 in concert. The girls couldn't wait. The up and coming band was taking America by storm and it would be the highlight of the warm months for each girl. Brandon was a senior that year and only took them because their mom told him he could use the car if he did.

"Josh and I aren't sitting with you and Lindsey," he told his sister, adamant about where they would meet when the concert was over. Rachel didn't care. It was more exciting to be off with her best friend anyway. "But don't tell Mom we let you go off on your own. I promised her you'd both stay with us."

Rachel and Lindsey looked at each other and shrugged their shoulders. What Mom didn't know wouldn't hurt her.

The two girls spread their blanket out on the lawn of the outdoor concert venue and instantly made friends with two boys sitting next to them. Their names were Frank and Andy.

Rachel took to Andy instantly. He had short blonde hair and surfing shorts. She wanted to be the California girl and he was definitely trying to be the California boy. They flirted on the blanket throughout the concert. The boys somehow had gotten some beer although the girls had no interest in drinking. Rachel knew better since her brother could be somewhere watching even though she doubted it. He probably had his own girl by now.

During U2's "40," what could only be a ballad U2 style, Andy reached over and kissed Rachel. She didn't tell him that it was the first time she'd been kissed by a boy. Or at least by a boy she wanted to be kissed by. She wasn't counting the time in fifth grade when, on a dare, Mikey Marshall had kissed her.

At the concert, this was the real deal, alcohol enhanced or not. Lindsey and Frank were taking it much further beside them but Rachel didn't look. They'd compare notes when they went to bed giggling at her house.

Several days later, Rachel received another letter from Jenny. "I showed your photo to everyone and they say you look like an American," her new friend wrote. Rachel wasn't sure what that meant but she chose to take it for a compliment.

She learned more about Jenny and Jenny had also enclosed a photo of her standing in front of their house in Coolum. Rachel repeatedly stared at the picture. If she looked like an American, did Jenny look like an Australian? What did an Australian look like anyway? Olivia Newton-John was one. But Jenny had short dark hair. She was heavily involved in gymnastics at one point although now she was into track and field, mostly the field events thanks to her arm strength from gymnastics.

Jenny stood near a palm tree that stood slightly taller than her next to a white house. They were just blocks from the beach. Rachel fell backward on her bed, sighed, and dreamt up ways to land herself in Australia. All she could think about was winning the lottery and she was still too young to play.

Rachel tried to imagine what Coolum looked like. Jenny told her about the sandy beaches, the surfing they did each day, and how the bus that took her to school drove along the road that lined the ocean. What was that like to see the ocean every day on your way to school and on your way home?

Instead of writing back this time, however, Rachel sent an audiotape back to Jenny. She wasn't sure where she got the idea but it seemed cool that they could listen to each other's voices and experience more of their lives that way. A whole 90 minutes at one time. She did admit it felt a little weird talking to herself though.

Rachel started hers by talking about the U2 concert, which was also the first concert she attended in her life, and the first kiss she experienced with Andy. The boy whose last name she would never know. Looking back, Rachel wasn't sure how she filled up a 90-minute tape because when Jenny sent one back the next time, she complained constantly about not knowing what to talk about. She was sure to mention Rachel's recent concert adventure though.

She told Rachel about the fun they had on the beach, a boy named Lance she was dating, and how cute he was. "I'll send you a photo," she insisted, "next time."

Green with envy. Rachel wished she could hang out on the beach. It had been her dream and she saw her friend doing it. But Jenny saw that Rachel had it made. She lived in the United States where many television shows and pop bands reached stardom. Everyone knew about the American dream.

By the time Jenny's tape arrived, school had started. It took several weeks for the girls' letters and tapes to travel back and forth across the Pacific Ocean. Rachel had a sense that her world had changed. She loved knowing that Jenny was out there and that when she came home from school or tennis practice, there might be a letter waiting for her on the kitchen counter.

"Some day, we're going to visit each other," Jenny had said in the tape. "I'm going to visit you and you're going to visit me."

Rachel longed for that day, hoping it would be after her high school graduation. What better time? she wondered, than before they went off to college. It would be her dream come true.

There was a lot to do in the meantime though.

Chapter 4

Rachel knew there was something about morning television, and television in general, that people didn't realize. Once the person left the studio, they had no indication whether or not anyone had seen the show. She was on her own until dinner when some people from the Australian arm of the publishing company would take her out before the book signing.

While the world might be watching, it's just you and the crew, Rachel thought.

Back at the hotel, she took a shower to remove the makeup and make her board-stiff hair somewhat soft again.

Miranda had said, "You know," as she looked at the back cover of the book, "I'm not sure that this is how I pictured you."

Rachel wanted to explain to Miranda that she was the temporary creation of Miranda's makeup and hair people. In the shower she had to remove the board-stiff hair and makeup to find herself again.

Rachel took a walk to get her bearings on where she was. Although she really wanted a nap, she knew that would be a mistake. She would have time to sleep later that day.

She had a map with her and thought it was time she saw what King's Cross was about. Along with the opera house, King's Cross was the only other part of Sydney she'd heard about. And it wasn't very good.

The publicity people had picked the hotel which was fine by Rachel. Sometimes she liked the notion of just showing up and not having to take the time to book the place. But in her curiosity, she looked online to get an idea of where she was staying. And in a travel review someone had noted it was near King's Cross which was "filled with hypodermic needles." Rachel felt a little puzzled since all the other reviews didn't give that indication. Everyone seemed to think the hotel was in a good place.

"Maybe it was a bad day," she mumbled to herself before turning her attention to something else on the Internet.

On this early afternoon it was time to check out these supposed hypodermic needles though. It reminded her of when she and Tom had gone to Mexico for their first anniversary. Right there along the Pacific coastline were several needles taking up space on the beach as if they were seashells. It was enough to keep Rachel out of the water for several days.

"Come on," Tom begged her. "At least come down and stand by the water while I go in."

"I'm not getting HIV from a needle on our vacation," she snorted back. "We've only been married a year. I don't want to end it now."

"Ow!" he called. Later he would tell Rachel that the look on her face was price-less. She feared the worst, that he had stepped on a needle. But as she came flying down the beach, he fell in the water laughing.

"Got you down here, didn't I?"

Rachel walked up a hill in Sydney thinking about how there were two perspec-tives to take on that. One was that maybe Tom's cancer came from an errant needle in the water. They truly didn't know what really caused cancer, did they? But the other side was that maybe Tom had been right. Maybe he un-consciously knew something that she didn't. Maybe he knew their time was shorter, of the essence, people would say. He could have had an inkling that they didn't have the fifty and sixty years that some couples enjoy. They had seven.

King's Crossing disappointed her. She wouldn't have any good stories to take home and tell everyone. It was a little funny to see signs that said "Legal Show Girls" but it almost felt like Times Square. And even some parts of Las Vegas. Plus there wasn't a needle to be found. Rachel wasn't even sure what she was looking for any way. She'd read it had been filled with mansions in the early 1900s although she didn't find any on her walk that the map listed. Rachel followed the crowd she was in and kept walking. Surely all these people knew where they were going.

The hills went up. And went down. How could Sydney be so hilly? she won-dered, feeling like she was in San Francisco. Or even Los Angeles. But the eastern coast of the United States didn't feel like this. She saw a park up ahead and walked through it, enjoying the grass and the trees. In the middle of the park sat an aquatic center consisting of several indoor swimming pools looking out of place.

That's when she stumbled on the church.

In front of Rachel stood St. Mary's Cathedral, a typical older church with a steeple and stained glass windows gracing each of its side walls. She walked inside and listened to the familiar sound of the wood plank flooring creaking below her. People streamed in and out. Rachel always wondered about the people who visited churches. Were they Catholic like her and taking advantage of paying homage to someone or something? Or were they just curious on-lookers like she might be if she were traveling through a place checking out a church of another faith.

Rachel knelt in a pew and said a short prayer. While she didn't go to church often, she did stop in them sometimes when she drove by. She always thought of it as a way to get closer to Tom. She didn't tell anyone that because she thought they would think she was silly. Why would she need a church to be closer to Tom? He was with her all the time. He sent her signs. He helped her write. The lights flickered while she wrote on her computer at night. Once a photo of his parents had fallen off a table without being provoked. That she saw as a sign that he was still annoyed with his family for not being there when he was sick.

That was one part of his dying she hadn't been able to control. She did everything she could but she could never get his parents to come see him. Or his sister. He'd worked hard as an architect and Rachel thought he was the most incredible man in the world. His family hadn't thought so though.

"Their loss," she always told him when he got down about it.

If he left his life with one regret besides never getting to drive a race car, that was it. But Rachel knew that it would be their bigger regret in the years to come when they would realize they were too late to love their son and brother. In those moments, she hugged him tighter and gave him an extra kiss to remind him of how she loved him and was grateful that his parents had brought him into the world so that she could share her life with him. Even if it was a short-ened version.

Here in the church, if she felt closer to God, maybe then she felt Tom could get her messages that she still loved him. But did it really matter? He knew, she knew. And he was telling her that she needed to keep moving forward, that he was pulling away from her so that she could have something new.

"What?" she wanted to know. There was no answer to that. And no signs. Or was she missing them?

Rachel got up and admired the stained glass windows before she spotted the candles off to the side of the church. It wasn't until Tom got sick that she started to light candles in church. While her mother often stopped at church when they growing up, she never told them what lighting the candles was about. They only thought it was exciting to see the flame and to watch their mom leave that flame in the church with all the others.

But now she had a chance to light one for Tom on the other side of the world. Not that that mattered where it was. She'd do it anyway though. It was for her.

The squat votives were difficult to maneuver into the tall glass holders. As Rachel went to set hers inside it, the flame from the candle to the left scorched her hand. She couldn't cry out. She grimaced with a little pain. Someone was reminding her that she was alive, that she had feeling. Was it Tom? She rubbed her hand lightly and shook her head. Maybe it was just his way of telling her that he was here. No, he wouldn't singe her hand. This was a reminder that she was alive.

As she began to walk away, thoughts came to her about the manuscript. She didn't know where they came from but she had to write them down. That's when she realized she had left the hotel without her bag. It was in the hotel safe. Instead, she had brought with her just the essentials: her passport, her wallet, and her hotel key. And the Sydney map of King's Cross.

Rachel panicked. She didn't want to have to remind herself of these ideas throughout the next hour before she went back to the hotel. It meant brain work with keywords and she'd been up too early that morning to do that. Plus she was still confused about what time it really was. Her cell phone stayed on Kansas time and a glance at it told her what was happening at home.

She remembered they had envelopes in the pews for people to send donations. She thought she would grab one and saw there was a little store at the same time. She could borrow the manager's pen. Surely he would let her do that.

The store was somewhat noisy with people almost pushing each other out of the way for their Catholic artifacts: rosaries and saint cards. And a Pope Benedict pen! Rachel giggled inside. Oh, the fun she could have with the pen. Surely someone in her family would want it. "Look at my Pope pen!" she would taunt them. "And it's from Australia." Her Aunt Shirley would be the first in line. She was the only one in the family who found Pope Benedict to be handsome in some way.

"Oh he scares me," she remembered her mother saying. "Something about those eyes. Shirley never did pick handsome men."

Before she could leave though, the rosaries caught her eye and she tried not to push the elderly couple out of the way to get one. Some were made of metal pieces rather than wood, plastic, or glass beads. It felt comfortable to hold one with metal beads. And it seemed right to buy a rosary here in a cathedral in Sydney.

As she walked to the counter and handed the man her pen and rosary, she said, "I needed a pen."

He scribbled on a pad to check that it worked and replied, "Yes, and they are rather inexpensive as well."

Before Rachel left the church, she sat down and wrote out her thoughts. Now she could relax and go on her way.

When she walked outside the large wooden doors, she realized just how high the church sat above street level. Coming up the stairs earlier on the way in had made her miss the view of the city laid out in front of her. And the park. But more importantly, it was like re-entering the world after taking care of some spiritual work. Maybe that had been their intention when they built the church.

She looked at her watch and started back towards the hotel to get ready for the rest of her book-related day.

Book signings always were a good time for Rachel. She had been lucky that her first book somehow had made it up the bestseller list quickly enough that she never had to experience signings where no one showed up. She'd heard horror stories from her work colleagues, but she also realized that some of them didn't think Rachel's writing was literary enough.

Rachel didn't care. She connected with people and that's what it was all about in her eyes. Her fellow professors didn't sell any books because they were too literary. Rachel didn't see how the average person could read, or would want to read, some of what they wrote. If they wanted a successful book, it had to be written in a way that people could connect to it. She knew she could have gone that route but she wasn't into writing a book that no one would read; she wanted to know people were picking them off the shelves and taking the time to spend with her characters. There was nothing more rewarding than someone saying, "Last night I curled up with one of your books under a blanket by the fire as the snow was falling."

After a sushi dinner, she and the three publicity people based in Sydney showed up together at the book signing. Quite a few people were already gathered there and Rachel took a deep breath before she walked inside the bookstore. She felt a little jet lagged still but she knew these people were looking forward to meeting her. And she hoped one of them was Jenny.

While Jenny's family had lived several hours north in Coolum Beach and then in Brisbane, the last address she had for them, there was no telling where Jenny lived now. Rachel had gone away from her own hometown in Michigan since she was now living in Kansas. Twenty years had gone by. A lot can happen in that time.

Rachel scanned the crowd of mostly women, from their twenties into their fifties, and wondered what Jenny looked like now. She had short dark hair and a great smile. That's what Rachel remembered. But there was only the one photo of Jenny in front of her parents' house in Coolum. Again, twenty years had gone by. She could have completely changed in that time.

And Rachel thought she had. She knew she wasn't the same person who wrote letters to Jenny twenty years ago. At least she hoped she wasn't. She hoped she was more secure for one. Writing to Jenny had been great. When Rachel was having a bad day, she knew she always could spout off a letter to Jenny and something about it would make her feel better. She thought it had to do with letting go of whatever she was feeling.

And she looked different now. The short bobbed hair of the '80s had been replaced by long straight hair of the new century. Less work, she always joked with her friends. Looking back, she wondered why she spent as much time as she did on hair and makeup. But maybe it was part of the security. When she became more secure in herself, she didn't need it anymore.

"I can't tell you how much your books mean to me," the first woman in line said after Rachel had done a reading and some Q&A with the audience. "I haven't been through anything like your characters but they always remind me of people in my life who I have watched go through life experiences."

Rachel smiled and chatted with each person.

"We're so glad you came to Australia!" several women cried out, giddy with meeting Rachel. "We brought the whole book club tonight. We've read all of them. When will the next one be out?"

Bah! Rachel thought, remembering the last conversation in the hall with her colleagues about reading. Wasn't it better that people read her books than not at all? And wasn't it better to write something that people enjoyed rather than not read at all? She had gotten better about letting it go. The people at the book signing proved she was right.

"I don't know why you don't quit teaching," her friend Tanya kept saying each time Rachel would bring it up. "You don't have to work this hard anymore."

Rachel knew the answer to that but didn't want to tell Tanya. If she did, it meant Tanya would try to set her up on more dates. Better to bite her tongue and let it go.

The questions continued. The praises kept coming. By the time Rachel left the bookstore with Todd, the publicity guy from the publisher, she was feeling pretty tired.

"No drink for you?" he asked, a slight smile coming out of the corner of his mouth.

She looked at her watch. She was leaving for Melbourne tomorrow afternoon. She could sleep in. "Let's go," she said, knowing the publisher was paying for any wine she might drink. They should for as well as her books were selling.

"Quite a following," Todd said, getting comfortable with her in a bar a few blocks away.

"Yes. I had no idea it was like this in Australia," Rachel laughed. "Maybe I should move here."

"We'd keep you busy but then I suppose there would come a time when you'd need to create something new."

"That's the second part of my trip," she reminded him. "That's where I go when all this is done."

"Watching tonight though, I find it amazing how much those women feel like they know you. They act like they sit on your porch and look into your windows." He pushed his glasses up his nose.

Rachel pulled her black shawl tighter around her arms. "I know. But that's the beauty of it. I mean, how many people get that opportunity in life? That's what writing is to me, creating something that people can relate to and feel they know you. But the reality is, they only know of you what you've created on

23

paper." She took a sip of her wine. "They typically don't know what I like to do in my spare time. Or that I make margaritas on Friday nights and have my friends over for homemade burritos. They just get what's on the web site. And what they ask me in person."

Todd was thinking. "So what you're telling me is that you don't reveal your whole self."

"I don't think I should. That's what keeps them coming back. And I don't have to worry about paparazzi." She shrugged her shoulders. "If I revealed everything about me, then you wouldn't have any work to do. There wouldn't be anything left."

Todd was still listening. Rachel could see the wheels turning in his head as he processed everything she told him. "I work with some really stupid writers," he admitted. "They are rude and they don't get it. But you are one of the great ones. You get it. You understand what your role is. That's great."

At least I got something right in my life, Rachel thought. But it's been a long road to get here.

*****

She drifted off to sleep easily that night. It was a long day and she still felt confused about the time. Rachel had left the rosary out next to her laptop and she grabbed it as she climbed into the king-sized bed. She began to feel strength from it. She didn't know how to explain it but it gave her strength she felt she lacked. Maybe it was because she had a sense that Tom was pulling away from her. She had to find it somewhere and the metal beads held it.

Rachel promised herself in the morning she would look up the prayers for the rosary. She remembered some of them but the ones that started it left her baffled, the ones that were closest to the cross.

And she laughed at herself. She hadn't felt much of a need for anything religious throughout the past six years. But now she was reaching out. And halfway across the world. Something definitely had to be changing inside her. Too bad she couldn't write about this internal struggle she was having. Mostly because she couldn't put it into words. She had no clue what it was about.

24

Chapter 5

Getting back on a plane didn't feel like a great idea, but Rachel once again packed up her stuff and continued on with her nomadic week. She was disappointed she hadn't made it to the Opera House but something told her that she'd get there eventually. She didn't have time to dwell on it with a flight to catch. Rachel would be glad when she arrived up north where she could throw her clothes in a pile and not have to worry about repacking them for several weeks. She thought the long trip had made her slightly crabby. Or maybe it was the jet lag talking.

After leaving her big piece of luggage at the bag drop, barely making the 23 kg limit, she still had over an hour before her flight was set to take off. She wandered around debating if she wanted to eat something or would rather wait until she got to Melbourne.

While Rachel debated, she stopped at the bookstore, looking to see if there was something she might want to read on the plane. She had a few books but thought maybe there was something she couldn't get in the U.S. that could be interesting.

Before she could reach into the newsstand though, there was *Summer Bay* right in front of her. It took Rachel by surprise. She stood for a moment and stared. Then her eyes darted back and forth as several women, pulling roller bags behind them, contemplated buying the book. One did. Another put it down and kept looking. Rachel debated saying anything to them. Should she?

No, she thought, better to be anonymous. But she hadn't expected the book to be in the airport. The book had been out about six months in the states already and any airport displays were long gone. They were waiting on something new. Sometimes it took a little longer overseas though, the rights and all.

Instead, she quickly walked past the newsstand without buying anything and continued her walk to the gate. She settled into her seat on the plane, thinking about how in less than a month she would be back home in Kansas. Summer would be in full bloom. And it would feel as if the trip had flown by. She would have about two months to get the manuscript ready for Marian.

"Rachel's team" she liked to call them. She had an agent, an editor, a lawyer, and a publicity person. She wished one day she could get them all in a room and thank them for helping her get to where she was. Some day, she thought.

For a moment, she closed her eyes and wondered what was going on in Kansas while she sat on the plane in Sydney on her way to Melbourne. It was still the evening before. It was too early for lightning bugs. The nights were still cool. When she would get home, they'd be out in full force though. Her friends would want to come over and hear all about the trip. They'd sit out on the back patio and laugh until midnight with whatever stories Rachel would have from her trip although she already knew King's Cross would not be one. The church, yes, needles, no.

They would expect some of these stories to end up in her novels. Rachel knew they would but the stories still had to reveal themselves in front of her. As did the internal struggle of Melinda and her fellow main characters in the yet-unnamed manuscript.

She thought about the concept of time. So many times, Rachel would start a tube of toothpaste and, before she realized it, she was squeezing out the last bits of it. She'd think about how she thought it was just full. Where did it go? How many days had passed since she had started it? How many teeth brushings could she get from one tube?

It was the same for this trip. Right now the tube was full, but before she would realize it, the time would have escaped her and she'd be on a plane bound for the United States again. And she hoped it would be filled with memories and several hundred pages of a manuscript.

*****

As she had been warned, it was cool in Melbourne. Rachel arrived late in the afternoon and needed to find dinner before she settled in for the night. She took a walk along the Yarra River next to her hotel. There were more restaurants than she would have time to choose from. But it was early and she decided to walk for a bit before turning back to choose one.

It felt like London or Scotland. Or one of those countries that Rachel remembered from an earlier book tour. While *Summer Bay* hadn't taken off in Europe yet, Wishful Thinking, her second, had and they sent Rachel there one summer to promote it. If the boots had been a crisis in Australia, they were an international incident in the UK. It was June when Rachel arrived. She didn't expect it to be warm nor did she expect the sun to shine. But surely she could wear her sandals and capris.

As the plane landed, it poured rain. And when she got up the next morning to get ready for her media appearances and then the first book signing, it was still pouring rain. She put on her walking outfit and slipped her ipod into her jacket and went out for a walk anyway.

She felt strangely out of place. Everyone was wearing black.

"It's like February in Kansas City," she muttered to herself.

Surely they knew she was an American in the crowd. And when she continued to wear her capris and sandals, she felt bad for the people there, wondering if they owned anything other than black clothes and black umbrellas.

Now in Melbourne it was the same.

It isn't that cold out, she thought, but then reminded herself how in the fall when the new semester started of the school year, she was always glad to wear her new fall clothes. She watched a group of rowers glide along the river and a few leaves twist and twirl in the wind on their way to the ground. The weather wasn't that cold, almost like a late September day in Kansas. Indian Summer always came and warmed it back up again around the first of October though. Still, it felt good to be outside and watch everyone.

And maybe the conflict would come by watching the people, she hoped, walking into a restaurant and asking for a seat outside where she had a good view of the people walking or biking home from work that afternoon. They each had a story. What were they?

In Melbourne, she was given directions to show up at the ABC, the Australian Broadcast Company's building, for a radio interview the next day. Rachel had been booked on "The Robby Allister Show."

"You booked me on a man's show?" she had laughed when the publicity people told her.

"He actually took the bite!" Julia laughed right back. "I think he's hoping to drum up the number of women in his audience."

Rachel sat outside the studio waiting to go in, watching a guitar trio perform. This would be a little different than television. They were anticipating callers.

It's all good, she thought. And it's Australia where they don't let anything bother them. No worries. It helped her understand Jenny and the great outlook she'd always had on life in their letters and tapes.

Robby sat her down across from him and they quickly set her up with head-phones and gave her a bottle of water.

"This is a cinch," she waved him off when he started to explain what would happen. "I'm just glad to be here. And happy to have a man interviewing me."

"I thought I might try some women's fiction for a change on my show," Robby joked, the commercial coming to an end. "Might let everyone see my softer side."

The show started much the same as all the others did, just a unique twist here and there that made each different from the last one. Somehow they all ended on her writing career.

"I see that you're a professor of English at the University of Kansas," Robby noted, adding the usual, "Yes, the home of Dorothy of the 'Wizard of Oz.'"

Rachel had learned to play along earlier in her career and take advantage of any Kansas humor. "I realize we're not in Kansas anymore," she reminded him.

"Are you a Kansas native?" he wondered, looking down the information that the publicity people had emailed him.

"Kansas City...Missouri." She smiled and Robby laughed. "But I'm a Michigan girl."

Before they went to commercial to take a break before bringing callers on the air, Robby had one more question. "I think all of us non-writers want to know how you became a writer. Was this something you always wanted to do?"

Rachel laughed. She knew this one was coming. She readjusted her headphones and dove in. "I always wanted to be a writer but I never wrote much other than what I had to do to become an English professor. I think it became easier to explore and study what other people wrote. And I had a life and a husband and my writing slipped away in that time."

But there was the second part to this. She always knew where to put the pause, just as there were people who stopped ironing at this point and looked up at the radio, wondering what it was that made Rachel pursue that writing career. Or turned up the radio in their car as they were driving through traffic.

"I lost my husband to cancer seven years ago. Once we found out he had pancreatic cancer, he only lived about six months. And it was after his death that I realized it was time for me to get serious if I was going to have that writing career I'd always wanted. I didn't have him anymore so I poured my grief into *Runaway Heart*. And I think you can read the rest of my history on Google."

"I'm sure there are quite a few tears being shed in the audience now," Robby said, taking a deep breath.

It would be a moment before the irons were picked up again. Or the brownies got mixed until they were ready for the glass dish they would bake inside. Or the latte got picked up again for another drink. The radio station in the car wouldn't get changed until she went off the air.

Rachel's life caused people to pause. And people connected with her story. They bought her books because of what she said on television or radio. Or what they read about her on the Internet or in a newspaper. Sometimes it was just reading the back of the book in an airport bookstore.

After the book signing that night, Rachel felt a little drained. It was okay, she told herself. The vacation was coming in the next morning. She would fly straight to the Sunshine Coast and sit on the beach for over three weeks and work on the new manuscript.

But before she went to bed, she again pulled out the rosary she bought. She had forgotten to look up the prayers that morning. There was time for that though. She hadn't had one since her mother bought her one for her first communion. That was somewhere in one of her boxes of history.

This rosary was different though. Her reasons for buying it were different. She took it in her hand as she crawled into bed. She wasn't really interested in saying prayers with it yet, she realized. That day would come. But for now, just fingering the metal beads gave her a sense of peace. Maybe it was because they took her back to the church where she had felt that peace. Or maybe it was because she needed something that she related to faith to keep close to her. Whatever it was, in some way she realized it was about Tom. That was okay as long as he was leading the way. Even if he was letting go. He was leading her to the rosary and her faith so that she would have the strength to go on as his presence in her life shifted again.

Chapter 6

Before leaving Melbourne, Rachel stopped to buy postcards. She had several friends who begged her to send at least two on her trip. And since she hadn't done it in Sydney, she thought she better start in Melbourne. She found a few touristy shops at the airport and was debating on which scenes best represented what she had seen when a lime green alligator caught her eye. A stuffed lime green alligator.

Rachel picked him up and thought he had been made with cashmere. He was cuddly soft. She debated for a few minutes, then grabbed the alligator and her postcards and went to the cashier.

"Oh he's so soft," the woman said.

"I know, I'm getting him for my niece," she said.

She let the alligator's head hang out of the bag throughout the flight. What lured her to buy him, she didn't know. Her brother's daughter Ellie would love the 'gator. But Rachel wasn't sure she would let Ellie have him.

*****

The plane to the Sunshine Coast was crowded. Annoyingly crowded, Rachel thought. She tried to hide in her book. She put her ipod in her lap which would allow her to turn it on as soon as they reached 10,000 feet. But that wouldn't be soon enough with that baby crying on the other side of the aisle.

She sighed and sighed and sighed. At least it was better when the plane took off. The engine roared and stifled the sounds of the women behind her laughing, talking about their boyfriends and the party weekend they were going to have. Rachel was happy for them.

But she was tired. And she couldn't let anyone know. What if they read her books? She didn't need to end up cast out as a diva on a web site. She just needed a little rest from all the people she'd been around the last few days. It had been great. She was grateful for her fans. She still couldn't believe that people enjoyed reading her writing that much. But it had worn her out emotionally. And she probably was still tired from the hubbub of ending the semester and getting papers graded and grades submitted so students could graduate.

Now it was time for a break.

Rachel picked up the headphones in the seat pocket in front of her thinking she might try the music on the plane first. She tried to untangle them but somehow it wasn't working. She felt like the person who had wrapped them into the package did it that way on purpose so she couldn't get them undone. She finally felt better when the plane's engines roared and it charged down the runway. Goodbye, Melbourne, she thought. Maybe I'll be back again one day.

Rachel watched her plane ease its way up the coast, enjoying the vast space that lined the shore where no one had placed a house or a building of condos. Australia still had a sense of openness although her experience had been that people expected it in the outback, not along the eastern coast. Rachel didn't need to see the outback. She felt the openness looking down on the water and the rocky shoreline. The South Pacific Ocean sparkled blue and green. It looked fresh and untouched with so little life along much of the coast.

The environment had changed by the time the plane arrived at the Sunshine Coast. Rachel then understood why people were so happy. It was like being on a plane from the Midwest to Florida in November. The sun shone happily and everyone knew shorts and seashells were just a short drive away. She hadn't expected such a different climate in Australia, often forgetting the vastness of the country geographically. While the temperature in Sydney had been comfortable, it was more like ocean side weather at the Sunshine Coast.

She felt more at home in Queensland. She wasn't sure if it was her outfits or simply the warm sun brushing her skin but as the cab drove her to the Sea Cabana Resort in Coolum Beach, she was just glad to be there.

*****

Rachel and Jenny sent several tapes back and forth before returning to letters. What made letters great was that Rachel could work on them no matter where she was. If she wasn't passing notes between her friends and herself at school, there might be a letter from Jenny to answer. The time between letters got a little longer as the girls were busy living their lives as high school students and typical teenagers. Later, Rachel would realize that she documented much of her high school years through writing Jenny. And if only she could get her "side" of the story she wondered what it would say. There had to be a lot she had forgotten.

Rachel had a crush on a boy on the football team named Terry. He was a sophomore and he and Rachel ate lunch together everyday. When Rachel reflected back on that relationship, she wasn't sure what she shared with Jenny but at the time it felt like the most important part of her life.

And Jenny had her own boyfriend, having moved on to a guy named Mickey. By now, the girls were into their sophomore years of high school and turning sixteen. Jenny was already driving but Rachel was learning. Rachel had long moved on from Terry. It hadn't gone very far in the first place. They continued to eat lunch with a mutual group of friends but advancing past a kiss hadn't happened.

Jenny was a different story though. She and Mickey had gone much further than Rachel had with any boy. Rachel wasn't sure if she was happy for her friend or embarrassed by it. If anyone in Rachel's circle had made it across home plate, she wasn't aware of it. She knew she wasn't ready to go there herself.

Or maybe that was Australia.

*****

In the darkened room, it took Rachel a moment to remember where she was. But as she lay in the bed at the Sea Cabana Resort, she relished the fact that the motion had quit. All the running from taxi to taxi, studio to bookstore, and the planes between Sydney, Melbourne, and the Sunshine Coast had worn her out. She was happy to be still. Finally, she could relax and sit until it was time to go home. If she chose to.

It was still dark and she glanced at the clock to see that it was 4:15 in the morning. The sun wouldn't come up for almost two hours. But how much rest did she give herself before she began to think about conflict? And what about the search for Jenny?

After rolling over several times, thinking how small she felt in the bed, and that maybe it would be nice to share a bed that size with someone else, Rachel realized she was sharing it with someone else. The alligator. She found him lying next to her. At first she wasn't sure what the soft funny-shaped lump was until she remembered the green gator. He definitely wasn't going to Ellie.

She placed him on her chest. No one had to know she was sleeping with a stuffed alligator. At home it was a stuffed yellow Labrador dog. No one knew that either. She'd rather have a real dog but didn't believe she was home enough for the dog to get the care it deserved. But now that she had bought an alligator on a trip to Australia, she was going to re-think that.

Rachel wasn't sure where that put her psychologically that she was sleeping with a stuffed animal. The yellow lab hadn't been a gift from Tom. She'd picked him up at the grocery store on a bad day. She was grieving. She was sad. She was angry. She thought she was feeling too many emotions at one time. And she wasn't sure how much hope she had for her future. She needed something to comfort her. At the time, a stuffed animal seemed to be just what she needed and she was right. His name was Carrots, since she'd found him near the carrots in the produce aisle. She figured a kid had picked him up in the gift aisle and Mom made her put the stuffed animal down in the produce aisle when she discovered her child carrying it around.

Something was bugging her in Australia and that's why she'd bought the alligator. She couldn't quite put her finger on it though. Life was good. Really good. What was she missing that she thought a stuffed alligator could give her? And a rosary from a faith that hadn't been important in her life since she and Tom had had a Catholic wedding all those years ago?

Light was showing signs of coming through the windows, urging Rachel to get up for a walk on the beach. With the sun coming over the horizon, several people dotted the packed sand with dogs but mostly it was quiet, the ocean lulling everyone along.

Rachel thought about how insignificant people are when standing in front of the rolling water. But what struck her most about the South Pacific was the clear blue-green crispness. As the sun continued to work its way across the sky the water became greener. And clearer. Rachel stopped to think about the importance of how the water and sun are connected. But wasn't life like that as well?

When she returned to the resort, she opened the sliding glass doors to the balcony and saw the man on the balcony next to her drinking a cup of coffee.

"Good morning," he said. Rachel smiled and waved back, wondering if he had traveled the night before, hadn't slept well, or had been out all night. He didn't look comfortable with getting out of bed. His wavy hair had arranged itself in all directions and he hadn't shaved in at least a day. His t-shirt was rumpled as if he'd slept in it for several nights or worn it for several days and threw it on a heap at night to put back on in the morning.

She walked back into her unit and opened her laptop at the bar where she had a great view of the ocean over the tops of the trees where the dunes separated the beach from the rest of Coolum Beach. It wasn't much of an ocean view but she selected this place because it was supposed to be quiet. And she could walk to the beach. That's all she needed.

On the bed, she spotted the alligator.

"I think I could use someone to talk to," Rachel told it, setting it on the bar next to her laptop. She ripped the tag out of the alligator's ear. "Oops, I'm sorry. I'm sure that was painful."

The tag read that the alligator's name was Charlene. "Are you sure you're a girl?" she asked it, the alligator staring back lazily. She didn't turn it over to check knowing full well there was no proof available on this stuffed version. "I think you're a boy so we'll name you Charlie."

With Charlie guarding the laptop, Rachel made her coffee and sat down to work.

But it wasn't easy. She didn't know the conflict. She wasn't sure what to write yet. Instead, she gravitated to her bag, looking for the rubber band with the letters. That felt like something more concrete she could work on. She could read them for a while. At least until the conflict showed up.

Chapter 7

It surprised Rachel how quiet the beach was. The South Pacific Ocean appeared serene in many ways to her. She wasn't sure if it was the absence of high-rise hotels and condos ("They keep raising the heights," the cab driver had complained on the way to the hotel) or the lack of people. Two men surfed and she stopped to take a photo, wanting to catch them.

But after watching for a moment with her digital camera held up to see them, a thought of panic came over her. What if something happened to them? What if one of them got caught in a wave and didn't come back up? She didn't want to have documented that. She put her camera away and kept walking.

There weren't many shells on the beach but it was hard not to look down. Rachel wanted to both look down and look up. How could she manage to do both? She couldn't get her mind to rest that there would be many walks along the beach over the next three weeks, to the point that it might feel commonplace for her. Or even boring. She doubted that though. The beach was too different from the cornfields and suburbia of Midwestern Kansas.

When she came to the main beach, near the center of town, she walked up to the street and looked for somewhere to eat. After getting a meal, she needed to do some grocery shopping but for now she wanted food. Pizza sounded good and she sat down at an outdoor café where she could watch both the people in front of her and the water across the street.

Coolum felt still since it was fall in the Southern Hemisphere. That was fine with Rachel although she admitted she felt somewhat out of place because it was spring at home. It made Rachel think Christmas was around the corner. And like she missed summer.

After ordering a personal-sized pizza with olives and pineapple, she pulled out her small notepad from her bag and made a few notes that had come to her while she was on the beach. It had been what now felt like a cinch to write the previous novels. Why was this one not coming together? She strongly believed that things would weave together as they were supposed to but something wasn't quiet clicking for this one yet. It never occurred to her that it might be because events still needed to happen for the rest of it to fall into place.

When Rachel looked up, she saw a man walking by and smiling at her. She smiled back thinking it was nice of him. But also that he looked somewhat familiar. It wasn't his shorts or his t-shirt. Or even the flip flops. He had wavy brown hair and his sunglasses perched on top of his head. Who was it? She wondered.

That doesn't make sense, she thought, I don't know anyone here.

He walked over. "You're in the condo next to me, aren't you?" he asked, standing above from where she was sitting.

Rachel felt like a little kid as he towered over her. "I almost didn't recognize you without your cup of coffee," she admitted.

He stuck out his hand that connected to his well-muscled arm. "I'm Jamie Stephens."

"Rachel Monroe, " she said sticking hers back out at him. And the connection was made.

"Are you getting something to eat?" he asked.

"Yeah, um, do you want to join me?"

He pulled out a chair and sat next to her where he, too, could see the people and the ocean. "You don't sound much like an Australian," Jamie said.

Part of Rachel couldn't believe how Jamie made himself at home, like they were old friends who hadn't seen each other in a while.

"No," she laughed. "I'm an American. But you sound like an Australian."

"That's because I am," he said. She liked the ease of his smile. It made his face light up. And it felt comfortable. "I'm on holiday from Sydney. I try to come up here about this time each year since it's pretty quiet. It allows me to recharge the batteries."

"Do they need recharging?" Rachel wondered, the waitress coming around and asking Jamie for his order.

"I work as an estate agent," he said. "I buy and sell houses for people," he added after she looked slightly confused. "It gets crazy. Fall is a good time for a rest."

The waitress returned with a water for Rachel and a coffee for Jamie.

"How about you?" he asked. "Are you on holiday?"

She took a sip of her drink. "Well, I had some work to do and now I'm here to rest."

"Work in Australia?"

She nodded. It was coming. She would have to explain who she was. Rachel sometimes felt a little weird about it. But with men, they weren't as impressed as the women who read her books were. "I did some television. Some radio. I came for a few book signings."

"You're a writer?"

Rachel smiled. "Most people don't believe me. I don't know what you have to look like to look like a writer," she joked. "I guess I should wear glasses rather than contacts."

"Have you written anything I might know about?" He leaned forward.

"Oh, mostly women's stuff. I did the Miranda Connor show the other day if that's any indication."

"All those housewives who need their celebrity gossip each morning?" Jamie laughed. "My ex-wife used to watch that show."

"Well, maybe she saw me this week."

The waitress placed the pizza in front of Rachel. "We'll have your order in a moment," she told Jamie who nodded.

"Go ahead and eat," he said, pointing at the pizza. "I'm not sure about that combination though."

"My favorite," she said with a smile, grabbing the first piece and savoring the melding of pineapple and olives. "It means I don't have to share."

Several minutes later, the waitress placed a meat pie in front of Jamie.

"And what's that?" Rachel asked. "One of those meat pies?"

"They're okay here but they're even better down the street. I'll take you there. How long are you staying anyway?"

"Three weeks."

"All here?"

She nodded, covering her mouth since she hadn't finished chewing her food. "I'm supposed to be working on a manuscript. I have until the end of the summer to finish it. I teach at a university so we try to schedule most of my writing work in the summer along with my book signings. It makes for good beach reading for people in the states."

They continued to talk and eat their respective meals. Rachel had been on her school schedule for the year which made it strange to have this much free time. Usually she was dashing off to teach a class or meet with a student between grading papers and working on some of her own writing. The little writing that she did during the school year.

When they got up to leave, Jamie asked her if she was heading back to the resort. "I need to go to the grocery store," she pointed toward the corner where there was one in a small strip mall.

"Want some company?" he asked. "I probably should get a few things myself."

In the store they went their separate ways. Rachel bought fruit and snacks for breakfast the next few days. She knew she'd get tired of eating out and eventually would be there to buy meal makings but not today. It was nice to think about having someone else cook, even though it was a restaurant, for several meals.

They walked the road back to the resort. It was the first time that Rachel saw the road and when a school bus filled with uniformed students passed by, she couldn't help but stare and think that's what Jenny had referred to in her letters. Rachel was on the road that Jenny had taken to and from school. The same one that ran parallel to the ocean.

She and Jamie talked mostly about what they did for a living and how they spent their time. Rachel learned that Jamie loved to surf.

"It calms my soul," he said, taking her bag of mandarin oranges from her when she switched arms. "There's something about trying to become one with the ocean."

"Is that why you come here?"

"Mostly. It's become my home away from home. But work is in Sydney. I come up for weekends if I have some extra time."

"It's a nice place to come to."

Back at the resort, they passed the pool and walked up the three flights to their landing. He handed Rachel her bag of fruit and they parted at their doors. "Maybe I'll see you in the morning on the balcony?" he asked.

"If you're lucky," she teased.

"You're the famous writer; it would definitely be me being the lucky one."

And with that comment they each walked into their respective condos. Rachel wondered what was going on in Jamie's mind, but she giggled at the few hours she just had. She had lots of men friends at home. It wasn't that she lacked dates. Time just hadn't brought her a meaningful relationship filled with intimacy and emotional sharing. She hadn't been looking for it either.

But about twenty minutes later, after she had unpacked her groceries and sat down to get the notes she made at lunch and spin them into pages of writing for the novel, there was a knock on the door.

It was Jamie.

"I was thinking about grilling some fish tonight by the pool. Would you want to join me?"

"Sure, that would be great. Can you give me a few hours to do some writing?"

He nodded. "The tide is coming in and I'm headed to the beach now anyway. I'll come get you when I'm ready."

Rachel shut the door and giggled again. Australia was turning her into a giggly girl. No one would believe her.

*****

When Jamie came by for her around 7:00, Rachel had written ten pages. She was surprised how quickly it had gone. The notes from earlier, the inspiring thoughts from the beach, had helped. Still no conflict. She was doing a good job setting the scenes around it though.

The resort was quiet, not much bustle this time of year, the manager, Jeff, had promised her. That was fine by Rachel. That's what she needed.

"I got some snapper," Jamie said, "fresh off the boat this morning. That's one of the best parts about being so close to the ocean. Fresh fish."

"If you can cook it," Rachel added, remembering that fish hadn't been her forté. "But maybe if I didn't live in a Midwestern land-locked corn state, I might be pretty darn good at it. Steaks are more my thing."

And it wasn't that she loved steaks. Tom had loved steaks. She was more a pork chop girl but she'd learned to grill a steak better than most, to the point where Tom suggested they stay in because she could cook them so well. That had been to her advantage when he was sick and it was too much work for them to go out. She had filled the freezer with steaks in those six months because that usually was what he craved. When he reached the point where he couldn't eat anymore, Rachel found herself left with a few and it took her almost a year before she could finally eat them. Having steak without Tom didn't feel right.

"Well, then maybe we'll have to have a barbecue," Jamie said.

They sat next to the pool to eat and Jamie leaned back in his chair. "You've been in Australia almost a week? What do you think? Are we what you thought we'd be?"

"A crazy bunch of partying people?" she asked, raising her eyebrows. "No, you're much more normal than that."

"Good thing."

"Actually, when I was in seventh grade, I had a pen pal from Australia. For some reason, I'd always wanted to come here," Rachel said. "I'm not sure if you ever had the tv show, 'The Love Boat,' but there was one episode where Julie, the cruise director runs off to Australia to get married."

Jamie leaned forward again. Rachel felt like he thought she was the most interesting person in the world.

"I was probably eight years old when that episode came out. But something about Australia entranced me then. And it wasn't the opera house. I just knew I had to come here. So when I had the opportunity to get a pen pal here, I nabbed it."

"Now I know why you're a writer. Are you still in touch with her?"

Rachel shook her head and took another bite of the potato. "That's what's strange. We wrote all through high school. It was awesome. We had plans to meet each other, to visit each other after we graduated. We wrote letters, sent audio tapes, the whole deal, back and forth. But she stopped writing during our senior years of high school. I don't know what happened."

"Where did she live?"

"Part of the reason I came to Coolum was because her family lived here when we first started writing. And then they moved to Brisbane. I wanted to go to the places she wrote about although I don't have any plans to go to Brisbane. I didn't want to be landlocked while I was here. I can do that at home in Kansas."

The wind came up, ending their dinner early. They cleaned up their dishes and took them to Jamie's condo. "Do you want help doing the dishes?" Rachel offered, handing him a stack of plates.

"Oh no, it's okay," he said. "I wouldn't want you to think Australian men can't clean up."

"Well, I guess I'll go now. Thank you," she said, feeling a little awkward standing in his condo and not really knowing him very well. Hadn't she just met him about ten hours ago?

"Thanks for joining me for dinner." Jamie walked Rachel to the door. "I'll see you on the balcony."

"Which might be later tonight!" she laughed.

This is silly, Rachel thought, I can't be thinking what I think I'm thinking. There's no way. That was a long flight here. She looked at her cell phone which kept local time to Kansas City. She didn't know anyone who might be up at 3:00 am. She'd have to block her insecurity herself. Maybe that was why she was in Australia where home was in the middle of the night. It forced her to cope on her own.

At least she could send her friend Tanya an email. Not yet, she cautioned herself. Rachel realized she could be totally wrong.

She grabbed Charlie and turned the television on. She was on vacation, after all. The writing could wait for the next day. Heck, she thought, maybe there was something to learn from television that might help the manuscript. And she had gotten ten pages down. That was a good start. It didn't matter. She lasted twenty minutes before she couldn't keep her eyes open anymore for the night.

*****

While Rachel saw Jamie the next morning drinking his coffee after his morning surf, she kept a low profile. She knew she needed to get some writing done. And she knew she had no excuses. Surely, Jamie hadn't come to Coolum expecting to meet her and spend a bunch of time with her anyway. Plus, some writing had come her way. She found herself taking notes furiously to assure that she didn't let go of what was impressed on her brain.

She took a break in the late afternoon and walked down to the pool. While it appeared people were staying there, Rachel still hadn't seen anyone but Jamie. Someone's laundry was hanging out on a balcony from another building but that was the only sign of life. She slipped into the water quietly.

Gliding across the empty pool, Rachel thought about her characters. She thought about the conflict that she still hadn't nailed. But she had enough work to do to keep her busy for now.

Don't panic, she told herself, it will come when its time.

She heard the pool gate squeak behind her and flipped around to see who it was. Being alone at the resort was getting easy and she wasn't sure if she wanted to share it with anyone.

"Hi," Jamie said, taking off his flip flops and dunking his feet in the side of the pool.

"Hi," Rachel said, swimming over to where he sat. They were under the canvas tarp that protected the shallow end from the potent Queensland sun. "What's the tide doing?"

He shrugged. "It's out until morning now. I'll get up early. How did your writing go today?"

She gave him the thumbs up. "I had a good day. I thought I would take a break."

"Have you had a meat pie yet?" he asked.

Rachel laughed. She had seen the signs everywhere she'd been but had yet to indulge in what she thought was supposed to be an Australian delicacy. "No, but I'll be happy to eat one."

"How about a walk into town for dinner?"

"That would be great." She got an idea as she answered. "Remember I told you about my pen pal who lived here?"

He nodded.

"Her family moved but I have her address when they did live here. Do you think you could show me where the house is? I thought you might know since you come here more often than I do."

"I'd be happy to," Jamie said, getting up. "I'll see you at 4:00. We'll do that first before it gets dark."

They walked along the road discussing politics on their way to get meat pies that evening. "Oh, I hate to go there," Rachel insisted. "It always gets me in trouble."

"But everyone discusses American politics," Jamie said.

They walked past the town center and Jamie instructed her where to turn right. And then another left. Rachel held one of the letters from Jenny. She noticed that the street they had turned onto was Cove Bay. She had the address memorized at one time. Jenny's street. While her family had long moved, Rachel thought it would help her place some of Jenny's life if she saw the house in person.

"Here it is," Jamie said, stopping in front of a two-story white house. Several cars were parked out front in the driveway.

It looked like any other house in Australia. It looked like any other house on the street. It had trees in front of it and lush green grass. It was up the hill a little as well and Rachel figured there was a good view of the ocean from the inside.

She opened the envelope to get the photo that Jenny had sent in that letter. It was her standing in front of the house.

"That's her? In front of the house." Jamie sounded impressed.

The trees were smaller, the shrubs almost petite. But twenty years had gone by. It was still the same house. At the time, it was Jenny's house. And here Rachel was visiting where Jenny had lived. Yet there was no Jenny.

"Okay, we can go," Rachel said quietly. "I don't want to scare anyone who is inside."

"Are you sure you don't want to knock on the door?"

Rachel shook her head, turning away already to walk back into town. "No, they moved to Brisbane in our junior year."

"But maybe they know something?" Jamie offered hopefully.

Rachel still shook her head and listened to her intuition. "It might have been sold several times already."

Jamie nodded and agreed, leading her back to the town center for the meat pies at the café he'd been telling her about. They sat in a corner booth by the window. It was early and they were the only two patrons in the small restaurant. Their food arrived quickly.

Or at least it seemed quick, Rachel thought, wondering if it was because there didn't seem to be anything called time when she was with Jamie. It was as if everything went on hold except their being together.

"Did you grow up eating these?" she asked, trying not to make a mess while she talked and ate at the same time.

"My mom can make them like you wouldn't believe. And I still get them for lunch a lot of days. There's a place not far from my office where the shepherd's pie is incredible. But when I come up here, I indulge on the chicken as much as I can. Or the fish."

Rachel dipped a fry into the ketchup and enjoyed every minute of where she was and whom she was with.

Jamie wasn't about to let go of Jenny for the night yet though. "Do you have any idea why she might have stopped writing?"

Rachel shook her head. "I have no idea. I wrote several times and never heard back. At first I thought maybe it was because of the mail service so I wrote again. I thought maybe the letter didn't get here. I think I sent several more after that."

It had been frustrating not to hear from Jenny. Rachel missed telling her the adventures of her life. And hearing about Jenny's life. At some point she had to give up and let it go. But she also knew that some day she'd make it to Australia and hoped maybe she could find Jenny then. Something inside of her kept her from completely giving up even though she had put Jenny on the backburner for what she called "The Tom Years."

"Did you do a Google search?"

Rachel nodded. "I have all her family member's names. I have her family's addresses. I've Googled and searched. And found nothing."

"It's almost like they don't want to be found."

"I don't know. Some people you can Google and they don't come up. It's the nature of the life they live, I guess. I'm all over the Internet," she laughed. "Googleable is what they would call me."

"I'll Google you," Jamie teased. "I still have to go to a bookstore and check out the back cover of your book to make sure you are who you say you are."

"If I had a copy on me, I'd show you. Of course you could use the Internet here."

"Didn't bring the laptop," he confessed. "I try to be out of touch as much as possible when I'm on these trips."

"You're smart. I can't leave home without mine."

When they returned to the hotel, she invited Jamie into her condo to show him the web site the publicity people had created for her. "And we can resolve this once and for all," she said.

"Well, it sure looks like you," Jamie admitted, teasingly sizing her up between the photo and what she really looked like.

Rachel laughed, getting off the stool to get a glass of water. "I don't know why you didn't believe me. I think it would take a lot of work to make all that up."

"But you're a writer, it should be easy."

Chapter 8

The next morning, Rachel wasn't going anywhere. She couldn't write. She felt antsy. It wasn't writer's block. She just couldn't settle into a rhythm. This was the first time she ever tried to write away from home. At home, she would get up and pull some weeds in her yard for a while. Or she might clean out a cabinet. Whatever she would do, it would allow her mind to wander and fulfill her physical need to get something done. Vacuuming worked sometimes as well. The ideas would start to flow and she could go sit back down again and get to work. There had been several times where she left the vacuum cleaner in the middle of the living room because she hadn't wanted to lose her train of thought. She'd remember it a few hours later when she would re-emerge from her office looking for a drink of water or some iced tea to urge her on for the rest of the afternoon and she'd trip over the vacuum cleaner on her way to the kitchen.

It took Rachel a few minutes to figure out what to do. She looked around the little condo. She already had been for a walk early in the morning. In fact, she'd felt really good and thought she would be able to get going quickly. She had deceived herself though.

Pulling on her bikini, she grabbed her book, sunglasses, and a few other things and headed for the pool. She hadn't seen Jamie that morning and figured he was off surfing. Or he was sitting at a café getting breakfast.

They hadn't talked much about his life but Rachel thought about how their lives paralleled yet not that closely. He and his wife had chosen to end their marriage. Or at least she guessed that's what had happened. Tom had died. They were both alone although for different reasons.

Jamie didn't appear to be lonely. He had a full life from what she could gather. His cell phone rang periodically when they were together although he didn't answer it. "Unless it's an emergency or my kids, no one gets my calls when I'm in Coolum," he had said. "I've been coming here enough years that everyone should have figured that out by now."

Rachel inched her way back into the pool via the sloping edge of the shallow end. The pool had been set up like the beach, for kids, she knew. She sat down in the middle of the slope and let the water and the sun wash over her. It was quiet enough that she could hear the swells from the ocean from where she sat muffled by the few cars that made their way down the road that ran in front of the resort.

She still had enough scenes to write in the book that she could get away without the conflict. The conflict had to come to her soon though. After all, what novel didn't have conflict? It was the basis of all fiction, something she had learned early in elementary school. Novels and characters developed because of conflict. She chuckled to herself as she remembered that it didn't always mean they progressed in a positive way though. Life is too messy for that.

Rachel was feeling like she was running out of time. She held her breath and slipped her head under water, careful to let her hair land on the back of her head when she came back up for air. There was nothing worse than wet hair that had no direction and landed wherever it wanted. A mass of impossible tangles. It had to at least be a sleek mess.

Leaning against the side of the pool, she thought about her character Melinda and all she'd been through and the eventual goal of the book. Rachel wasn't sold on the ending she had created either.

"Hi," a voice said, creating a shadow above her.

Rachel looked up and removed her sunglasses to see Jamie standing above her. He looked like he had just woken up from a nap. "Hi," she said. "I haven't seen you at all today."

He pulled a chair over from the table nearest to where they were. "I was really tired this morning," he said, pointing his right arm north. "I went out last night to Peregian Beach to meet some friends for drinks."

Rachel listened. She realized he had been gone the night before. If she didn't see him at night, it didn't seem to bother her yet it also surprised her. She was still glad to turn out the light before it even got dark. Maybe it was because she was too tired to care about anything but sleep when darkness set over Australia.

"I stayed out a little late but that's what holidays are for, you know?"

She nodded as if he was looking for her to agree. "I think you always have to have one night of lots of drinks on a holiday," she joked.

"But you haven't had yours?"

Rachel laughed. "I don't judge my vacations that way."

"How's the writing?"

She laughed again and ran her hand over the smooth edge of the pool, looking up at him. "I'm here you see. I couldn't settle down so I thought I'd come down here and see if I could get myself figured out."

"Writer's block?"

She shook her head. "That's never really the problem. I'm restless. I'm used to running around. My life at home is busy. That's why I can't really write more than one book a year. I know they'd like to see me do more but I couldn't do it. I just couldn't get myself settled down to work."

He didn't say anything so she continued. "I'm having problems with this book. I have the characters and I have so much of what I want to do, but for some reason, I can't quite get the main conflict to be exactly what I want it to be. Usually that's what starts me writing a manuscript but this one I'm going backward for some reason and it doesn't seem to be working." She shrugged her shoulders.

"You're talking about the climax and all that other stuff we learned in school?" Jamie asked. He slipped his feet out of his flip flops and pulled his shirt off, guiding himself into the water next to her.

"Yes, the same stuff I used to teach," she said.

"Not anymore?"

"Once you become a famous writer," and she put quotes around the word "famous," "they think you are finally above teaching English 101. It's either you become famous or you teach for so many years until the rest of the department has left or retired. I got lucky that my first book moved up the bestseller list and it was like, 'Oh, she knows something!'"

Of course that wasn't everyone in the department but Rachel didn't feel the need to share that part with Jamie.

Jamie swam to the other side of the deep end and Rachel turned to watch him.

"Suddenly, I got to teach the fiction workshops. And the upper level lit classes."

"Why did you become a writer?" he asked as she swam across to meet him now. The deep end of the pool wasn't that deep for Jamie whose feet touched the bottom but Rachel bobbed around by treading water.

"I wanted to tell stories." While she spent a lot of time with the people who read her books, as well as her students, talking with Jamie about her writing was different. He was interested for one. She had appreciated the many dates set up by her friends but the men couldn't quite grasp that Rachel's world was about telling stories about these people who ran around in her head until she got them down on paper.

Some of them thought she stayed in bed all day waiting for ideas to come and then the money rolled in. They didn't understand how hard she worked for what she had. She had built a career around teaching and the writing piece came second although it was slowly creeping up to taking over the teaching part of her life. In the summer, a few of them thought she could drop everything in the middle of the day and go to lunch. They just didn't get it. Nor did they want to talk about how she created characters and some of her struggles. But Jamie appeared like he wanted to listen and she needed someone to talk to.

"You know," she said, a laugh escaping her mouth, "when I took my first fiction class in college, I was a terrible writer." She shook her head, partly unable to believe she wrote so badly at one time. "I can only figure that it was my own insecurity coming out. I think I recycled every bit of that writing. I wouldn't want anyone to see that now."

She swam over to the middle of the pool where she could stand comfortably.

"When did it change?" He wiped the water off his eyes.

Rachel realized she had never thought about when her writing changed. When had she become more secure as a person? It took her a moment to think about it. She stared blankly at the water. Jamie waited. "You know, I guess when Tom died. I didn't have any choice but to be strong. I still had a lot of life and, even though he was gone, I hadn't died, too."

She hadn't told Jamie more than the simple fact that Tom had died. But he didn't flinch as she talked about him.

The more she thought about it, the more she realized that Tom's death had been a defining time of her life, more than any other she could think of. She had to be secure in herself. The world didn't stop. And she also knew he didn't want her to stop living.

"Go on, you're a beautiful woman," he had said before he was so sick he turned into an old man and his voice went rasp. "Make sure you get another husband."

At the time, Rachel couldn't even think about it. She couldn't imagine life without Tom. They had married to grow old together. She curled up in the bed next to him, as she did many times when he was sick, just so she could feel him breathing. When she was sleeping, there was no sickness. Sleeping was comfort and she did as much of it as her life would allow during that time. He slept a lot of the day and Rachel climbed in bed with him, even for twenty minutes, when she could. She did it even when she had errands to run or they were out of milk. She knew the days were numbered and she wasn't about to miss any time if she could help it.

"Will you get married again?" Jamie asked, interrupting her thoughts.

Rachel swam to the ladder and climbed out of the pool to sit on the edge. "When I meet him, whoever he is," she said with a shrug. "What about you?"

"My situation is different than yours," he said. "One day maybe. We'll see."

The need to write was coming back and Rachel knew she had to feed it while it needed feeding. "I need to go," she said, making a motion like she was typing on a keyboard.

He smiled and gave her the thumbs up. "Get to it while it's there," he said, urging her on. "I'll be next door. We can talk more later."

"Thanks," Rachel said, appreciating that he understood. She wasn't even sure that Tom would ever truly have understood. She had never gone that route when he was alive. Their lives had been too full.

Back in the condo she got to work and pumped out ten pages with ease. She felt somewhat emotionally drained when she was done but that was okay. Rachel walked out on the balcony with her glass of water and gave herself a pat on the back that she had pushed through and made it a more productive day than it looked like earlier. It went to show that sometimes getting out or doing something else was the key to getting her focus back.

She admired the ocean across the treetops and took a few deep breaths to relax.

"Are you done or taking a break?" Jamie asked, finding her sitting there.

"I'm done," she said, relieved.

"Then come over," he nodded, "I'm making some prawns and pasta. I didn't want to disturb you if you were still writing."

He was setting a place for her at the table when she walked into the condo. "You know, I should cook for you one of these days," she suggested. "Or one of these days before we leave." Sometimes when they were talking, she forgot there was an end to it. Maybe this was what her readers referred to when they didn't want the story and characters to end. Maybe some part of Rachel didn't want this time with Jamie to end. She stopped herself short this time and hoped he wouldn't notice.

If he did, he didn't say anything, continuing to serve up the shrimp and pasta with a salad. "I'm glad you got your writing done," Jamie said, handing her a beer and keeping one for himself. "If that's your goal for your holiday, then I hope you complete it."

Rachel took a drink from the bottle before she started to eat the meal in front of her. "You know," she said, before she took a bite, "we've talked all about Australia but I've never asked you if you ever wanted to come to the states."

"I did when I was younger. I think it was the same for any of us as it was for your pen pal. We all thought America had it all because of music and television and movies." He wrapped noodles and a shrimp around his fork and chewed them before speaking again. "But you know how it is when you're younger and you think the grass is always greener somewhere else. Sure I'd like to visit the states one day but I love where I live. And I love where I vacation."

She couldn't disagree with him. While she was very comfortable in Australia, almost too comfortable in some ways, she didn't know if it actually was a place she could live. She only could figure that her comfort came from knowing so much about the country from Jenny. Still, she liked home. Maybe she didn't have the ocean and the summers were brutally humid but she had a good job and great friends. She had a great life.

"You can go anywhere you want, you know," Tanya would say when Rachel would complain about the humidity in the summer. Or something about work.

Tanya always made it sound easier than it was. Rachel didn't see herself picking up and moving. She was comfortable, she admitted that. But Tanya was right, she could go anywhere she wanted now. She could get another teaching job. Or she didn't have to teach as long as she kept writing. No, that sounded too easy. She needed to stay where she was. She needed the comfort of familiarity. At least for now.

Jenny had sent Rachel a t-shirt in the first year they wrote to each other. Rachel had sent Jenny one as well although now she couldn't remember what it looked like. But the t-shirt that Jenny sent Rachel was sitting in her office at home. She couldn't fit into it now thanks to her late breast development in high school, but it brought back some happy memories. It had been in one of those boxes her mom had saved for her.

"Jenny sent me a t-shirt from Australia," Rachel told Jamie.

"Mmmmm," he said, eating more while looking up at her.

"I thought I was the coolest person in school because I had a t-shirt from Down Under," she laughed.

"Do you still have it?" He had finished his plate and drank more of his beer now.

"I do! I can't wear it though. I grew boobs after I got it."

Jamie laughed with her and got up to get more food. "Do you want anything while I'm up?" he asked.

"I'll have another beer." Rachel was glad to be finished for the day. She was proud of herself for pulling through. "I'm rewarding myself," she joked.

"Then you should," he said, tipping his bottle toward hers. "Here's to you finishing your writing today."

It felt good to be acknowledged. Rachel was used to pushing herself. Other than her team, no one else really knew much about she was writing or how to motivate her. When she was at a signing, people wanted to know about the next book as did the people who sent her emails and letters. And her friends would ask sometimes although they had learned that when Rachel was ready to share, they usually were the first to see what she'd worked on. They always waited patiently until she called them over and handed them copies of a manuscript and gave them a date to return it by.

"Thank you," she said, putting the beer down. "For your support."

"No worries," he said.

The second beer was just as good as the first. They were laughing and Rachel had a sense of peace within herself as the sun went down outside and another day ended.

When she went to help Jamie put the dishes in the kitchenette, she bumped into him. He was backing up from the sink and she was walking toward it. "Oops," she called out, trying to balance the dishes and keep them from breaking. He grabbed her wrists with his wet hands to help her balance.

"Whew," Rachel said, watching the glass on top stop shaking. She looked up at Jamie who was smiling down at her. She didn't realize that she only came up to his neck until that moment. Perspective, she thought, it's a different perspective of him.

They stood there for a moment and Rachel wasn't sure what that meant. Part of her wanted to lean up toward him and let him kiss her. But was that what he wanted? She didn't know. She thought it was better to get the dishes on the counter. And let it go.

Jamie didn't say anything. He released his grasp of her wrists and returned to washing the dishes. It was a little uncomfortable at first. Rachel turned around and took a deep breath, letting the beer know it wasn't going to have its way. Then she turned back to continue helping Jamie clean up.

It was the first time she felt how strong he was. Not that she didn't think he was strong; again, it was a change of perspective.

"Are you going surfing in the morning?" she asked, returning the towel to him after wiping down the table.

"I think so," he said. "I have to check the tides at the front desk."

Rachel leaned against the refrigerator and watched him finish the dishes. "It's been a long time since I've had someone cook so many meals for me in such a short period of time," she said. "I really think I need to make you something."

"You could do that," he agreed. "I wouldn't turn that down."

"Okay," she said, sensing she was getting tired fast. The sun had long gone down and that meant she was late for her early Australian bedtime. "Maybe tomorrow night if you don't have plans."

"It's a date," he said. Rachel's stomach fluttered when she heard the word "date."

As Rachel returned to her dark condo and climbed into bed, she thought about the definition of the word "date." If she hadn't been so tired, she would have looked it up. "Date" meant something more formal. Still, she had lunch dates with her friends. Maybe date meant something different to Australians though? Rachel's head was spinning and she took a deep breath to let go. She realized she needed sleep to think clearly in the morning. She held Charlie in the crook of her right arm and the rosary in her left hand. She knew if anyone could see her now, well, she wasn't sure what they would think.

She knew everyone thought she was the epitome of strength. She had accomplished almost more since Tom died than in the years before. To the people who didn't think she grieved though, they were wrong. That was her grief work; making her writing come alive. And it was what Tom asked her to do.

If people connected so much to Oprah Winfrey, then maybe, Rachel realized, she wasn't revealing enough of her fears in her life to her readers. Oprah was about revealing her faults, remarkably her weight loss, and how she persevered through them. But Rachel still didn't want to reveal too much. She wanted her protagonists strong although sometimes there was fear in their strength. Women connected with her main characters because they put their fears aside and trudged forward. She never got the impression they wanted to read about the women who curled up in bed all day eating chocolate when they were dumped by a man.

No, Rachel thought, I'm using Charlie and the rosary to cope. There's nothing wrong with that. It's not a sign of weakness. It's a sign of strength because they are helping me gain momentum and keep my momentum. Life is about moving forward.

She didn't think much after that. She drifted off to sleep and when she woke up, the rosary was under her pillow and Charlie was still in the crook of her arm.

Chapter 9

Before starting her daily writing, Rachel walked to the grocery store in town to figure out what to make Jamie for dinner. She got sidetracked when she looked down a road and realized there was a church there. She had thought she might want to find a church in Coolum to feed this sudden need she had to cling to religion. But the experience wasn't the same as what she felt in Sydney.

As Rachel neared the church, she knew it wasn't what she needed and didn't feel a need to walk inside. The rosary appeared to be enough for her. What she had experienced in the cathedral in Sydney had fed the need better than she realized.

Rachel turned around and set her thoughts back on dinner that night.

One of her favorite meals to fix, besides burritos on Friday, was fajitas. She knew she was pretty good at it, too. She thought if she could find all the ingredients, it might work. But she also needed a grill pan. Rachel searched the grocery store high and low after making a list. Cheese, chicken, onions, bell peppers, olive oil, and limes were easy. But she also needed tortillas, chile powder, and garlic.

A little guacamole always was good, too. She found tomatoes and avocados but still hadn't located the tortillas and the chile powder. She knew there wasn't such a thing as a true Mexican in Australia. They'd already told her that a Mexican to them was someone who lived south of the border of Queensland. That wasn't quite the same. A cheap grill pan would work and makeshift tortillas– they were for wraps but they were as good as she could get. She had searched the store two times before finding the wraps. They were hidden in a corner near the snack foods.

"These Australians put things in the oddest places," she had mumbled to herself at the time, thinking they would have been with the bread at home.

Her kitchenette leaned toward the primitive side. Rachel scratched her head for a moment and thought of her grandmother who never cared that her kitchen was small and that the family always gathered there anyway. She still made the best meals in the world and that's all that mattered. Rachel could do the same.

With everything marinating, she went back to writing, remembering all the cooking she had done until Tom died. Now it was just for her friends. It felt strange to be cooking for a man for the first time in what felt like many years. She laughed to herself thinking she was being dramatic. It hadn't been that long.

However, that was her past. Maybe cooking for Jamie allowed her a chance to remember what it was like to cook for someone again and push her down the road to being with an "other half" again.

She felt the corners of her mouth turn up slightly as she thought about what her friends would say when she told them she had cooked dinner for a man. An Australian, no less. None of them had emailed her and thus knew nothing of her trip at this point. They would wait until she arrived back home and invited them over for dinner.

One day she hoped she could let go of those final scenes in her mind of Tom in the last hours of his life. They didn't haunt her nor did they plague her. They still brought a mild sense of sadness that her strong husband had deteriorated into someone she barely recognized and could hardly speak in the end. It was like his soul was being sucked out of him and, as it happened, the rest of him shriveled up.

No, no, no, Rachel thought, putting her fingers back on the keyboard and taking a deep breath. I have to let go of those thoughts. That's not how I want to remember Tom. And he didn't want me to be stuck.

*****

When she was graduating from high school, it had been disappointing to Rachel that she wasn't going to Australia before she started college. She'd been planning and saving for the trip since she and Jenny had started writing and discussing how they would visit each other.

Because of tennis and school, Rachel only worked summers at a local pool taking tickets, but with each paycheck she put a little bit aside for her trip. Everyone knew she was planning to go Down Under. If she was given a chance to pick a place to write about, Rachel wrote about Australia or something else related to the country.

In the meantime, her life continued on. Tennis took up a lot of time and she continued to get better and better. Playing in college became an option and Rachel looked forward to furthering her playing career as well. The boys came and went, but writing started to take hold of her more than she imagined.

It was her American literature class in college where something challenged Rachel inside her and a spark flew that she hadn't been able to extinguish since. And it was Jamie who asked her about it when they were filling up on red wine and fajitas that night.

"Do you remember the exact moment that you wanted to become a writer?" he asked, unable to stop eating the food she had prepared.

Rachel was somewhat happy with it. While it wasn't perfect because she wasn't at home where she knew she could get flour tortillas or use her seasoned grill pan, it wasn't bad.

"It was several events," she told him, wrapping up her second fajita to take a bite. "In junior high, I had this teacher, Mr. Aronson, and he was so cute." She put her hand on her heart and made it flutter as if it was beating hard.

"So it was the teacher who started the writing career?" Jamie laughed.

"I think the storytelling aspect was always there," she admitted. "He just did a nice job bringing it along." She ate part of the fajita and then put it down to tell more of the story. "He had us write this story about crushes we had." She couldn't believe she was telling Jamie this story. It was an embarrassing one she had never told anyone. "So I wrote about how this girl was pulling weeds and she has a fantasy, nothing sexual, about how this man rescues her from the drudgery of weed pulling in the family garden."

"I would ask you if you're kidding but you're a writer so I know you're not," Jamie teased her.

By now Rachel was laughing so hard that she thought she was going to fall off her chair. "It's true," she said, catching her breath and wiping her eyes. "The thing is, Mr. Aronson never knew, or he never said if he did, that he was my fantasy. I would be weeding the garden in the summer and I used to dream that he would come and rescue me from it."

She finished her fajita and Jamie was laughing himself.

"But that's not the whole story. So when I get it back from him, he hands it to me and he tells me I've done so well that he thinks I could get into the fiction workshop program at the University of Iowa one day." She knew that meant nothing to Jamie. "That's a big deal."

"Did you?"

Rachel shook her head. "There's more to the story but I didn't go to Iowa because I went to Indiana. I ended up pursuing the literature end of things and I wanted to become a teacher. One thing led to another and I ended up with a doctorate. But there's more."

Jamie got up to retrieve the opened bottle of wine off the bar.

"Mr. Aronson was so cute," she said a little dreamily. "The man had such curly hair that we all would have died to run our hands through it. At least that's as much as a bunch of 13-year-old girls can understand." She let the memory go and moved forward while Jamie sat down to listen for more.

"When I was in college, I took an American Lit course. I couldn't even tell you that it was related to anything specific that we read, but we had to do a paper on the American dream. I remember being in the library, since these were the days before the Internet, and something lit up inside of me that to this day I still don't fully understand. It was like when we light a pilot light on a stove or a heater and it stays lit until something blows it out. I feel like that. My pilot light is still going strong.

"So I'm looking up quotes for my paper and it starts to grab me. I 'got' the educational process. I 'got' the pursuit of that dream. Something fell together and I felt unstoppable in the library, as if no one could control me when it came to getting quotes. And quotes that fell together into that paper."

She stopped and looked up at Jamie who wasn't saying anything. And she felt a little embarrassed. Maybe she had shared too much about her nerdy side.

"You don't get it, do you?" she asked him.

He had finished eating and pushed his plate aside to forward and be closer to her. "I do get it. I never had those same kind of academic urges but I'm guessing that it's much the same way I feel about surfing. It's about hitting that perfect wave just right. I'm sure that you are always trying to create the perfect story."

Rachel shrugged her shoulders. "I'm not sure that that's possible though," she said. "My mom makes quilts and she says that you can't always make the perfect quilt because only God can do that. So maybe only God can create the perfect novel as well."

"And surf the perfect wave?" Jamie asked. Rachel shrugged her shoulders. "But we can keep trying, can't we?" he asked. She nodded.

She removed the rest of her food from the wrap and ate it with a fork leaving the wrap behind.

"The wrap didn't work for you?" he asked, pointing at the rest of the bread-like circle that lay limply on her plate.

She stuck out her tongue. "That was not a good excuse for a tortilla. I know the only Mexicans here are those like you who live south of the border of Queensland."

Jamie laughed. "Where did you learn that?"

"I've been here a while," she reminded him. "I've picked up a few things."

"Okay, so you ended up getting a degree in literature then?" he asked.

"Yes. I actually got it in English because I knew I'd need a job that paid money and I figured the best way to do that was to become a high school teacher. But I never did teach high school. I ended up going straight to graduate school for my master's and then I ended up getting the doctorate after which I ended up teaching at the university level."

"And somewhere in there you got married?"

Rachel thought for a moment. "We met right after I started teaching. Tom was from Kansas and that's where we met because that's where I got a job."

"And the writing got left behind?"

"I don't know that it got left behind so much as I felt like I didn't need to do it at that time as I thought I did before. I love teaching. Although it doesn't happen all the time, there's something about sharing what you know with others to help them learn without realizing they really are learning."

Rachel picked up several plates from the table to take them to the sink in the kitchenette.

"Did you have any writing ideas during that time?"

"I squashed them," she said. "I thought they weren't valid."

"But at some point you realized they were?"

"When they wouldn't go away," she admitted. Not until she needed something to think about other than the fact that Tom was gone. But she didn't say that.

"Where do you get your ideas?"

"You want to be a writer?" she teased him as she filled up the sink with hot soapy water to wash the dishes.

"No, I can't write at all," he said. "About the extent of my writing is email and estate contracts. But each time I go to a bookstore or a library, it fascinates me that people have something to say and that they put it on paper and other people read it. And if I'm in a bookstore, I think about what it must be like go to in there and see your own book, something you created, on a shelf."

"And you hope it's not in the clearance pile," she teased herself.

"It doesn't sound like your books are," Jamie said, wiping down the table as she had done at his condo the night before.

"Not that I've seen it but if you go on Amazon you'll see how many are up for sale as used copies. That's the nature of it though. Not everyone will love it or want to keep their copies."

"Except the people who you signed them for," he said.

"And asked me a million questions about who I am and where I get my ideas from."

"Are you referring to me?" he asked. Rachel thought she saw a sparkle in his eye when he said that.

"You have asked me more questions than all of my fans combined. But you've also had more time with me than any of them have had."

"Bonus," he said, laughing. "So where do you get your ideas?"

She shook her head as she began to wash the dishes. "I couldn't tell you where they come from. They just come to me. And sometimes they're unstoppable. I have stacks of notes at home in a folder because they don't belong anywhere or to one project. But I feel like they have a home somewhere. I just don't know what home that is yet."

"And this one now?"

"This one is a little more complicated. I'm struggling with the conflict for it. I have all my people and I know what I want to happen but I can't quite figure out what her, her name is Melinda, conflict is."

"Can you tell me more about it?"

Rachel hated to disappoint him. "I can't yet. It takes away from the storytelling aspect if I do."

Jamie seemed to understand. "But there will come a point when you will be able to tell me?"

"I think the ultimate premise of what I write about is women finding their way in the world. It's like a healing journey with a dash of romance. I have to throw that in there. Everyone likes a sprinkle of romance, at least women do."

Jamie agreed.

"Much of life is figuring out who we are, what we want, where we belong. And I like to create strong women figuring that out."

"Do you ever use audio for your thoughts?" he asked.

Rachel continued to shake her head. "No, there's something about writing down my thoughts that's important to the process of who I am. Notes on scratch paper are a way to start and then actually typing them out." She lifted her fingers out of the water and dropped the dishcloth to act as if she was typing.

"I think it's incredible how you get it down on paper," he said, picking up a tea towel to wipe the dishes for her.

"You know you don't have to do that," Rachel told him, reminding him that he hadn't allowed her to help at his place.

"I figure if I stay longer, you'll keep answering my questions and I get to try and figure out what makes you tick."

"Don't you think it's time we talked about you?" she suggested.

Jamie laughed and opened the cabinet. "It's a good thing these are all the same," he said, putting the plates exactly where they belonged in his condo.

"Well, if you want to talk about me, for one it would be a fairly short conversation. And, two, that probably means I need to head back to my place."

Rachel didn't pursue it but she thought he was wrong. "We're all complicated," she said, leaving it at that.

Chapter 10

When Rachel woke up in the morning, Charlie's face stared back at her. She patted him on the head and rolled over to face the ceiling. She could see it was a little cloudy out and she hoped it would burn off by lunch so she could go swimming that afternoon. She still hadn't been swimming in the ocean but that was okay. Just walking along the ocean was enough for her.

When she walked out to the balcony with her coffee, Jamie had beaten her there.

"Tide is out," he said. "I was going to make you a coffee and deliver it to you but I wasn't sure when you'd be up."

"Wild night we had," she joked, settling into the plastic chair by the table.

"Are you going to walk?"

She nodded. "Once I wake up. Maybe in about twenty minutes."

"Can I join you?"

She nodded and took another sip of the coffee. Then yawned.

When she walked back inside to change into shorts and a t-shirt, she realized she had been sitting out on the balcony in her pajamas. A white tank top and short orange shorts. Really short. Rachel laughed at herself and thought about banging her head against a wall. What was I thinking? she wondered. I'm getting a little comfortable here. Jamie hadn't said a word though, nor did he look like something wasn't right. She realized that the reality was he probably enjoyed seeing her like that. A bikini showed more anyway, she giggled to herself.

She pulled on her shoes and began to tie them. For all those years she had wanted to go to Australia, now the trip was halfway over and it felt a little strange. Rachel was beginning to wonder what she would take away from it.

When she graduated from high school and she had saved all that money to go to Australia but with no one to visit, her parents balked at putting her on a plane to another hemisphere where she knew no one. Looking back at it now, she

63

realized she should have kept the money and gone one summer during college but tennis and work kept her busy.

A part of her had been angry at Jenny for stopping writing. They had made all those plans about what they were going to do when they visited each other. And then nothing. Rachel held out hope as long as she could. Everyone asked during her senior year when she was going. It was an exciting time of her life; she had a tennis scholarship to Kansas and had definitely decided to major in English by then. She thought her life was on the track where it should be.

But there was a piece missing. She so badly wanted to meet the pen pal who had been her confidante, who had served as her diary for four years. Nothing came though.

Rachel remembered coming home from school one afternoon; it hadn't been a great day. She hadn't done well on a math exam and was tired from tennis. When there was no letter on the counter, only another college recruitment envelope, she lost it and went up to her room and cried.

She kept writing Jenny. She just acted as if Jenny was still there, just hadn't had time to respond. Rachel realized that part of her needed something from Jenny because she did serve as that diary. But she missed two-sided aspect of their letter writing, she wanted to know how Jenny was doing.

Finished lacing up her shoes, Rachel plopped her sunglasses on her head and listened for Jamie's door to open. She met him out front and they set off for the beach.

While she still felt tired on her way out to the water, the sound of the waves and the salty smell revived her. She still loved to come through the woody path separating the dunes to see the water spread out endlessly in front of her. It made Rachel want to embrace life, just as Jenny always had. She thought of one incident where Jenny stole her parents' car to go to a party late one night. She didn't seem to have any fear of life.

"Life is meant to be lived!" Jenny had ended one letter.

"Let's go this way," Jamie said, looking off to the left. For some reason, she kept going to the right, south to the center of Coolum.

Something about the unknown kept her from going the other way.

That's silly, she told herself, you know life is too short not to explore all its roads.

"I think I've been here too long," she joked to Jamie. "I'm getting set in my ways of which direction I should go."

They walked as far as they could, meaning as far as the beach would let them. It was about a mile. Jamie climbed on the big black volcanic rocks where the beach stopped and held out his hand for Rachel.

"We're too old for that," she said, gulping after she said it.

"Just because we're not in our twenties anymore doesn't mean we can't do these things," Jamie reminded Rachel, his hand still held out to her. "Come on, I'll make sure nothing happens to you."

She trusted him and it paid off. They didn't go far but the view from above was incredible as the water washed up on the rocks. "Look at the clarity in the water," Rachel sighed, staring down at the sand that lay below the layer of water. "You don't get that too often."

"Now that you've been here a few weeks, what do you think? Is it everything you thought it would be?" Jamie asked.

"It sure beats Europe," she joked, telling him how she had saved all the money to come to Australia after high school but didn't go after Jenny stopped writing.

"What did you do with the money then?" he asked. "I'm sure that took you a long time to save with the kinds of jobs we all had in high school."

"I sat under an umbrella and took tickets for a swimming pool," she told him. "It wasn't very gratifying but at least I was outside. I had a tennis scholarship so I didn't need the money for school. I ended up taking a trip to Jamaica during graduate school with some of my friends. We thought we were really cool, four girls leaving the country together." She rolled her eyes at the thought. "It wasn't Australia though."

"When did you get to Europe?" They watched the water wash up on the rocks before it retreated, causing a spray that almost hit them.

"I got to go for one of my books a few years ago. It wasn't Australia either," she laughed. "I never quite felt like I fit in there like I do here."

"Disappointing?"

Rachel nodded. "Although I can be tentative at times, I do think I have done a good job living each day with as much energy as I can. But that was the one piece of my life that I couldn't quite make peace with."

She wasn't sure what she had done with the Australia dream. Maybe life had gotten too busy with college and tennis. And then graduate school. And Tom. It had been pushed aside like her writing. All those diary entries. Where were they now? Tossed in the garbage?

"I guess I wasted my time writing to Jenny continually even though she never wrote back," Rachel said. And then she thought for a moment about what she had just said. "But maybe that's not true since life does put us where we're supposed to be at any one time." She shook her head. "I don't know. Sometimes I don't get it."

"Maybe you aren't supposed to get everything," Jamie suggested. He had a stick in his hand and tapped it against the rock they were sitting on.

"This is really silly," Rachel said, a thought popping into her head, "but there was one reason I thought maybe Jenny had quit writing me."

Jamie squinted at her and pulled his sunglasses off his head and onto his eyes. The sky was finally clearing up like every morning.

"Her mom had this crush on the actor, whose name I don't remember in the tv show 'V.' It was this show about these aliens coming to America and how they tried to intermingle with the humans. I think it started as a movie. I don't remember him being that cute but, you know, her mom was older than us, what did I know."

Rachel laughed. "This seemed stupid now. Jenny wrote that her mom wanted information about this guy and that I was the only way they could get it because he was an American and it was an American show. I looked, although I'm not sure where I looked, and never found anything."

"And you thought that's why she stopped writing?"

She nodded. "Which is silly because that was before the Internet and Google. We didn't have the access to information that we have now. Now you could just Google the guy's name and come up with the information. I always thought they were mad at me because I didn't do the one thing they asked me to do." She paused and thought for a moment. "The mind of a high school girl."

"We better head back," Jamie suggested. "I think the tide is coming in and we might get stuck up here. Since it was my idea to climb up here, I better be the one to suggest we climb down."

She followed his lead and took his hand. But before she did, she took one last look at the view from where she stood. Surely Jenny had stood there at one time or another and thought the same things Rachel was on this morning: the massiveness of the sea, the importance of embracing life, the significance of hope.

Something had to have happened to Jenny. She wasn't the kind of person who stopped writing. While someone can be whoever she wants to be in letters, Rachel knew, that just wasn't Jenny. Why would they make so many plans together? Even mailing each other copies of their respective televisions guides so they could see what the other was able to watch on television?

Wherever she was, Rachel hoped she was okay. Her hope for finding Jenny was beginning to dwindle.

Chapter 11

"I have an idea," Jamie said, leaning over the balcony two mornings later. "I'm driving up to Hervey Bay for the weekend to visit some friends. I wanted to know if you wanted to come with me."

Rachel smiled. "That sounds great." Then she stopped. "Did you tell them you were bringing someone?"

"I told them I was bringing an American girl I picked up on the side of the road."

Rachel laughed. "I hope not."

"No, I said I was bringing a writer from America who needed to see more of Queensland."

Rachel laughed again. Back at home she wasn't sure if she would have done what she was about to do. Maybe she was crazier to do it in Australia. Life was too short though. And her time was on the downhill slide Down Under.

"You didn't have to do this," she said to him, watching the shoreline pass as they drove north in Jamie's car. It was a beautiful afternoon and the ocean looked crisp with the sun hitting it and turning it green and blue against the clear sky.

He ran his hand through his hair and smiled. She noticed a few grays peeking out near his ears. "We don't have to do a lot of things in our lives but sometimes when we throw things out there, even when we aren't sure how they'll end up, the best thing we can do is at least try."

"Do you think everything happens for a reason and that everything happens as it's supposed to?" She asked.

"I think you mean, do you believe we're supposed to be in this car heading to Hervey Bay right now?"

"Yes."

"Yes, I do. Even when we're in the midst of life events and we don't understand why we're going through them, we always can look back later and understand why we were put in a specific place at a certain time."

Rachel nodded and watched him search for another radio station as the one he had tuned in faded out.

While people had told her that they compared Queensland to Florida in America, Rachel felt like Queensland was cleaner. At least it felt cleaner. But maybe it was because she was in there in the fall, not during the spring or summer humidity. It had a lush freshness about it.

There wouldn't be any surfing in the quiet waters of Hervey Bay but Jamie didn't seem to mind leaving his board behind.

Rachel was a little nervous when they drove up to the house belonging to his friends. She imagined that they thought she and Jamie were together. Or had he been specific with them that this was nothing more than him offering to show her more of his country?

The couple walked out of the house as they drove up the long driveway that led to the house with a balcony that stretched all the way around it. Once inside, Rachel would understand that was so they could watch the water no matter where they were on the second floor of the dwelling.

Sara and Ken were a little older than Jamie. Their kids were grown and gone; they were school teachers in the local schools. Their faces looked a little weathered from living outside. But Rachel felt they were happy. They were content with their lives both together and apart. Something about them read that they were in the midst of middle age and were enjoying the heck out of it together.

She smiled to herself, knowing they appreciated how lucky they were to still have each other after over twenty years of marriage.

"Hi," Rachel said, sticking out her hand to them. "I'm Rachel ..."

Sara stopped for a moment while she shook Rachel's hand. "You aren't the writer are you?"

She laughed and looked at Jamie. "You didn't tell them who I was?" He shrugged his shoulders. "I didn't know who you were. How was I to know that Sara would?"

"Oh! You are!" Sara was excited. She turned to Ken. "She wrote *Summer Bay*, that book I was telling you about that I was reading last month." Then she turned back to Rachel. "I had heard you were going to be in Australia, but I missed you on the Miranda show the other day. Oh gosh, I can't believe this."

She took Rachel's hand and led her into the house. The children had once lived on the bottom floor and she guided them each to a bedroom with a bathroom in the middle. "I hope that's okay," Sara said, looking a bit embarrassed that she couldn't offer Rachel her own bathroom.

"No, it's fine, it's fine," Rachel laughed. "I'm not a diva. I'm just Rachel."

When they had settled in, they all met upstairs in the main living area of the house. Rachel walked out to the balcony to see the bay, sans the trees and several houses that blocked some of the view. It didn't matter to Rachel. She sat down on a chair and admired the view in front of her.

Sara followed her out with brie and crackers along with a bottle of wine and glasses. The men appeared several minutes later.

"What I want to know," Sara said, tossing her head back, "is how you stumbled onto Rachel?"

"Or do you mean how did Rachel stumble onto me?"

Rachel swallowed her wine hard to keep from spitting it out from laughter. She could tell this was going to be a good weekend.

"Our condos are next door to each in Coolum," Rachel said beating Jamie to it. "He started it."

"I stalked her at a café in the center of town and wouldn't let up."

Sitting there, Rachel realized how much she had missed being part of couple-dom, even though she and Jamie weren't really a couple. They were a couple of friends. But they had arrived together and would be considered a couple over the weekend and that was okay.

Sara though, had lots of questions. "Will you sign my books while you're here?" she asked, excitedly. "I can't wait to tell my friends. I'm going to have to think of everything I ever wanted to ask you and make sure I ask you before the weekend is up."

Her husband finally stopped her, his fingers touching the top of her hand. "Love, maybe Rachel doesn't want to discuss her work all weekend," he reminded his wife who looked like she was taking a sip of wine to slow herself down.

"It's okay," Rachel said. "I didn't write the books for me. I wrote them to share. I learn a lot from the people who read them," she admitted. "And I get ideas."

"See," Sara said to her husband. "We could end up in a book."

Later, Rachel poked her head in the bathroom later to make sure Jamie wasn't there. Following dinner, they had sat outside and relaxed while the sun set. It had been a bigger day than she had thought and she was looking forward to washing her face and brushing her teeth.

But as she placed her toothbrush in her mouth, there was a knock at the door but she couldn't answer it with her mouth filled with toothpaste, the tube in one hand, her other hand wet from holding it under the faucet to check the water temperature. In walked Jamie, Rachel grinning with toothpaste foam everywhere around her mouth.

"I'm sorry," Jamie said, backing up.

"Mwerewrwerwemmmew," Rachel said, finally spitting it out. "I couldn't let you know I was in here because my mouth was full."

"I see that," he said looking at the sink.

"I'll be out in a minute," she told him. "I won't be long." Before he left, she called to him. "Jamie?"

He looked at her. Rachel could see that he was tired. His eyes were a little droopy. The four-hour drive wasn't short and then they'd been laughing since then.

"Thanks for bringing me up here," she told him.

He smiled. "Sure."

But what she didn't tell him was why she really appreciated it. Jamie couldn't understand the road she'd been down nor would she expect him to. And that was okay.

Sara had asked Rachel if she wanted to go for a walk early the next morning. The tide would be out and they could spend some time together on the beach. Rachel knew that really meant Sara could ask her a million questions about her writing. But that was okay. She was up for it.

Heck, she thought, as pulled on her shoes, Sara might give her an idea for some conflict.

The two women headed down the big hill that led to the beach. Sara was chatty most of the way while Rachel took in the views. And there was so much to see on the beach. The tide was out but there was black rock everywhere.

"I had no idea there was all this volcanic rock here," Rachel sighed, mesmerized by the view. "I guess I never thought about it."

The tide had washed in during the night leaving shells, coral, and rock everywhere. Rachel wasn't sure if she should look up, down, or out. And then she saw some big pink fish.

"Those are red snappers," Sara said. "Sometimes they end up on the shore, other times, they get filleted by the fishermen who throw them back in the ocean." She sighed. "It's too bad but I suppose it's part of the food chain. The birds will eat them."

They rounded a corner and kept going, staying close to the water's edge where the sand was firm.

"This is amazing," Rachel said.

"And you'll see a whole lot more today," Sara reminded her, picking up a shell. "I'm sure Jamie is planning to show you around." She nodded her head and giggled to herself. "I still can't believe I have Rachel Monroe … at my house."

"Oh, I'm just Rachel," Rachel said, touching Sara's arm.

While it had started out cool that morning, it was warming up quickly as the sun came over the water and hit the land.

"I don't know what the status of you two is…," Sara started to say.

Rachel wanted to cut her off and tell her that there was no status. But she also wanted to hear what Sara had to say. She watched Sara stretch her arm as if it had cramped up.

"But it would be nice to see Jamie be with someone. He and Maria divorced four years ago. The kids were just three and one. It was traumatic for everyone involved but I think they realized that the kids were better off being raised separately by two parents rather than by two parents who hated to be in the same room as each other."

This was more information than Jamie had offered her, Rachel thought, taking it all in. She had tried to ask, to pry, but he had acted more content to talk about her. That didn't sit well with the writer in Rachel though. He had done a good job deflecting the attention but she'd get it back now. She was going to take control.

*****

The pier was incredible. It reminded Rachel of something out of a book that couldn't be replicated. She wasn't sure she could come up with the words to describe the scene. The water was almost smooth as glass and shallow. She could see several islands of sand.

And it amazed her how many kids were on the pier fishing with their fathers. And there was another group of three kids on bikes with their dad.

"I bet Mom sent them out," Rachel whispered to Jamie. "She probably said, 'Please free me for the day!'"

He laughed and they sat on an empty bench to admire the view. Rachel couldn't believe something so beautiful existed. And it was so different than Coolum. "It's getting easy to love it here," she joked. "I guess my intuition from the time I was eight years old was right."

"Yes, I believe it was. Australia is the best place in the world," he said, acting as an ambassador for his country with an official sounding voice that made Rachel laugh.

The kids on the bikes passed by, their dad right behind them.

"You have kids," Rachael said. He had mentioned them although she couldn't get him to say much about them. "Tell me about them."

Jamie looked a little uncomfortable. He looked away, watching an adolescent boy catch a small fish.

"Why won't you talk about them with me?" she finally asked.

He didn't speak at first.

"Why?" Rachel knew she had to get an answer now.

"Your husband died," he reminded her. "I know what you weren't able to have. I didn't want to rub in what I had and don't have now."

She was stunned. No one had ever said that to her before. "Wow," she said quietly, a gentle breeze blowing her hair into her face. "I had no idea you had thought that much about me."

He touched her hand. "Rachel, my ex-wife and I hated each other." He laughed although it wasn't a pleasant one. "I'm not even sure how Carly was conceived. Honestly, I was probably desperate after watching a night of footy, er football, with my friends and came home and crawled in bed with her. She wasn't conceived out of a night of love-filled passion like how our marriage started."

Rachel wasn't even sure how to react. And then she thought she shouldn't. She should let him talk because he might not say this much again.

"But I love Max and Carly more than anything in the world. I wasn't going to make them live with both of us hating each other. I wanted them to see what a good relationship is about." He shrugged his shoulders and looked at her. "And I know when the time is right, I'll find it."

Rachel felt a wave of nervousness come over her. It was as if Jamie knew something she didn't realize.

"See, I know your husband died. You never got to have kids. You and he loved each other right until the end. You don't even need to tell me that. I can hear in it in how you talk about him. I didn't want you to feel any anger at me because I let my marriage go."

"Oh Jamie," she said. "I don't feel that way at all." It felt like they were the only two people on the long pier. The kids and their dad and the bikes had long passed again on their back toward land. Fish were being pulled out. Other people walked by. But Rachel and Jamie didn't see anything but each other and the water and sky that surrounded them. "I learn so much from other people and their relationships. In fact, that's where I get most of my ideas. My first novel was published because I wrote what I was going through after Tom died even though the main character is someone other than me. Please don't be afraid to share with me."

74

And then she realized something. "But you said we should share more often than many of us do?" Rachel reminded him.

"I didn't say I was good at it," Jamie laughed, getting up and holding his hand out to her. "Let's go. I want to take you to see more of Hervey Bay."

Something changed for Rachel after that conversation. And it was all because of Sara. If she had been at home, Rachel knew that her friends would have been encouraging the relationship. But since she was so far away, and out of touch with them, it had been easy to set it all aside. And maybe it helped that Jamie constantly brought up Jenny. Rachel found she was too absorbed with everything else to focus on the possibility with Jamie. Besides, she reminded herself, he lived in Australia. It wasn't around the corner from Kansas.

But after the conversation on the pier, Rachel wanted to wrap her arms around Jamie. She wanted to tell him that he was a wonderful man and he deserved the most wonderful woman in the world.

While she didn't do that, she did come up with some ideas and dug out her little notebook from her bag to jot some of them down while Jamie drove over to the fish co-op where they could pick up a few fillets for dinner that night.

"It never stops does it?" Jamie asked, chuckling as he glanced her way where she was writing furiously before the several thoughts disappeared as if they had never been hers.

"Mmmm," she said, letting him know she'd be with him when she was done. He pulled into a parking place and she kept writing. When she was done, she flipped the notebook closed and dropped it and the pen back into her bag. "No, it doesn't."

They dropped the fish off at the house and Jamie told her he wanted to take her to one more place. Barums Head Beach. To get there, they had to drive away from the water and come out again on another side of the bay.

It was as if no one had ever been to Barums Head Beach. While there were houses across the street from the beach, the beach itself looked pristine. The clear sky let the water almost blend in with the horizon where sea and water met.

"After I got divorced, and before I discovered Coolum, I used to come up here and visit Ken and Sara and walk on this beach. I did a lot of my therapy here."

"Pretty inexpensive," Rachel pointed out.

"And much better looking than the witch we used to mediate our divorce," he said, a hearty laugh preceding it. "She had quite the nose."

"What kind of answers did you find out here?" Rachel wondered.

"I discovered much of what I had forgotten about myself. I had worked so hard to spend time with the kids, or it was just one really at the time, that between them and work and fighting with Maria, the surfboard didn't leave the garage for almost two years."

Rachel gasped. Then she remembered that was when she had given up playing tennis. When Tom got sick. And life was changed after he died. She hadn't played since. "I'm sorry, I can't picture you not surfing."

"That's because that's all you've seen of me. But that's the real me. I surfed so little after I got married. It had defined me for a long time but I guess I thought it was time to be an adult and surfing is never really looked at as an adult activity."

"You don't care now?"

He shook his head. "It's my sanity. I'm a much happier person. I'm sure it's much like your writing. It appears to me that you need to write because that's who you are."

"But it wasn't like that before," she admitted, holding a hand out to stop him. "I had always wanted to be a writer. At some point in high school I had decided that. But I was smart enough to know that I would have to make a living some how. And I was too busy living life to get anything down. I played tennis in college and majored in English and went on to teach. I got married, I kept playing tennis. I was teaching." She paused to dip her feet in the water and Jamie stopped next to her. "Then Tom got sick and all I could do to survive was take care of him. I wasn't going to give up any time with him because we weren't sure how many months or days he had left."

"When did the writing come then?"

"You coped on the beach?" she asked him, pointing her head at the sand under them. "I coped by writing. I poured all my grief into my first book. That's what made me the writer I am now. And I still haven't played tennis."

"You miss tennis?"

Rachel shrugged her shoulders. "Not really. It only defined me for a period of my life. It wasn't like surfing is to you. You're right, writing is what defines me. I need to write to be who I am now."

"And would you give up teaching?"

She laughed. "Everyone says I have enough money to do that but that would mean way too much time alone. I've lived alone since Tom died and I don't think I could just write and live alone, too. I'm much too social for that."

"Could you write and live with someone?"

"I think so, although I don't think it would be easy. You saw me jotting ideas down. I don't think I could ever have done that with Tom although he wanted me to write. It worked out in that time. I understand now that my writing career was supposed to come later."

They walked back to the car. Neither one had realized that it already was just about past lunchtime and Sara had said she would have sandwiches ready.

"Life puts you right where you're supposed to be," she told him, taking a drink from her water bottle.

After lunch, Rachel took a little time to do some writing. She wanted to get the notes she took into some form on the laptop just like the chunk of clay she was turning into a manuscript. She also knew that if she did a little as she went along, it would help out when she got home and needed to fill in the holes.

The door to her room was partially closed and she jumped when she heard a knock.

"Hey," Jamie said, leaning into the room. "Do you want to go swimming before dinner? We just took the solar cover off the pool."

Rachel smiled. "I thought you'd never ask."

"Wait, I don't want to keep you from writing," he said holding his hand out. He walked in and sat on the bed where she was working.

"You aren't and you won't," she said. "I know what I need to do and I won't be kept from living life either."

Rachel noted she was looking at him differently now. Was it because she was spending more time with him that she noticed the scars on his face? There was something about that one on the chin. She figured it came from a surfboard. Or was it because she saw him in a different light?

She stopped herself, it didn't matter. She only had two weeks left in Australia anyway. She couldn't get attached. "Now you better leave the room so I can change," she reminded Jamie who gave her a look as if a light bulb went on in his head and he got up to leave.

Swimming in the pool, Rachel's thoughts turned back to Jenny. The more Rachel saw of Jenny's country, the more she knew she was exposed to the possibility of somehow getting to her. Not that Australia was a small country, but Rachel knew that the world was always a smaller place than it seemed.

Somehow everyone is connected, Rachel thought, watching Jamie talk to Ken and take a drink of his beer. Sara was lying on a float, her eyes closed to the sun. She had just been saying, to no one in particular, that they would eat dinner around 6:30.

Summer always had been important to Rachel. There were two times of year where she felt the most hope in her life when she was a teen. One was when school started, probably because it was a new year which meant a chance to start over in some ways. Plus there were new experiences, new classes, new adventures in tennis. And the boys had changed over the summer.

But summer vacation also brought its own sense of newness as well. Rachel knew it was about possibilities. Each summer she was hopeful that it would be more exciting than the last one. She would wonder if there was a new boy to befriend at her local pool job.

She didn't have a boyfriend as often as Jenny did. Every letter Jenny either had the same boyfriend or a new one. Rachel was smart enough to know that it didn't have to be true. Maybe Jenny made them up. But she doubted it. Why would she? She was a pretty girl with a happy smile. But part of Rachel knew she was envious of that side of Jenny because Jenny seemed to have it all. And that "all" was what Rachel wanted but hadn't quite gotten.

It would take Rachel much longer to get where Jenny was at. She wasn't sure if it was her own insecurity. Looking back though, wasn't everyone insecure? It would take Rachel until her mid-twenties to feel good enough about who she was in life and somewhat secure in herself. Even with Tom, part of her was a little tentative. She often was the one holding him back. "Okay, Mom," he'd tell her, as if she wouldn't let him go down the big slide at the water park. But he wanted to do much more than that. He wanted to buy the most expensive car, the most expensive grill. He wanted it all right then and there.

Now that Rachel thought about it, Jenny had been much the same way. It was as if life came easier to both of them. And quicker.

"Are you in there?" Jamie asked, poking her in the arm.

Rachel looked over at him. "What?"

"Do you want a drink?" Ken is going to get more beers and he wanted to know if you wanted something."

"Oh," Rachel said, breaking her daze. "Some water would be great."

He pulled up next to her on the steps and placed the beer out of pool range, where the glass wouldn't break.

"Thinking about Jenny," she said before he could even ask. "I'm halfway done with my trip and I don't feel like I've done enough."

"I haven't helped," he joked.

"No, you've helped a lot," she said, skimming her hand across the top of the water. "I guess I just had some sort of fantasy that by appearing on radio and tv, she'd find me."

"Maybe she's a high-powered solicitor and doesn't have time for television," Jamie suggested. Rachel looked confused. "Lawyer," Jamie said, "in American speak."

Rachel knew the possibility was there. "I just thought even though it's a big country, she could easily find me since I'm all over the Internet."

"You still have some time," Jamie said optimistically.

"I know." Rachel wasn't sure what was left though.

Before dinner, Sara suggested Rachel and Jamie take a walk. "The kangaroos have been out lately and I'm sure you'll want to see at least one," she said to Rachel.

"She's right!" Rachel exclaimed when they came upon a male with several females just down the road where a small clearing met the woods. "It's just like our deer in the states."

They stood and watched them for a moment, mostly the kangaroos staring at the couple and the couple staring back. They didn't appear interested in hopping off. And they acted like they had homes nearby.

"I can't imagine being an animal," Rachel admitted. "I like living in a house. But I guess to them, the woods are their house."

"I don't think most people would like to sleep in the bush at night," Jamie said leading her down another road that would wind back to Sara and Ken's house.

The kangaroos had reminded Rachel of the time she and her friends went to the zoo in high school. They had a day off and someone suggested they take a trip there on a spring day. Rachel had been obsessed with the Australia exhibit. She had to see it. She waited patiently because it was at the far end of the zoo from where they came in. But as she waited and they meandered their way around the monkeys, the elephants, and the flamingos, the sky turned dark.

And then poured rain.

"Let's go!" Amber and Laura had called, covering their heads with their jackets as if it would make a difference.

But Rachel was adamant. "I'm not going without seeing the koalas and the kangaroos!"

They rolled their eyes at each other and then at Rachel. "We'll meet you at the car then!" They took off running one way and Rachel went the other way. She'd gone all that way and wasn't going back without seeing what she came for.

The exhibits were empty in the rain and that was fine by Rachel. They were all inside anyway, but the rain had sent everyone home. She watched the koalas sleep in trees and the kangaroos stare at her just as they did by the street in Hervey Bay. All by herself.

Dinner was another laugh fest. Sara had gotten over being star struck with Rachel staying in her house for which Rachel was grateful. She didn't see herself as some people did. She was still Rachel, sleeping with a stuffed alligator and a rosary now.

"In honor of Rachel being in Australia for the first time," Sara said, bringing out dessert, "I made sticky date pudding!"

Rachel looked a little confused. What she saw looked like a big bran muffin, or maybe a chocolate muffin, with a caramel topping. Did it have pudding inside? She wanted to ask but was a little embarrassed.

Jamie turned to Rachel who was on his left at the square table. "Sara makes the best sticky date pudding."

Ken laughed from across the table. "You don't know what it is, do you?"

Rachel finally shook her head and smiled.

"Do you mean that Jamie didn't get you any sticky date pudding in Coolum?" Sara lamented. "Well, I guess he was waiting for you to taste mine." She handed a plate to Rachel along with another fork. Jamie and Keith dove into theirs.

It wasn't pudding. It had a solid middle. Whatever it was, it was to die for, she thought. Butterscotch topping, too.

"What is it?" she finally asked.

"Oh, lots of butter and a few dates," Sara laughed, eating her own.

"And it sure beats those hockey puck muffins we got the other morning," Rachel reminded Jamie.

"Hey, you picked those out, not me. They weren't bad either."

Rachel stuck her tongue out at him and he grinned back. Something had definitely changed.

At breakfast the next morning, Jamie mentioned that Rachel had had a pen pal in "the old days."

Rachel laughed as she spread brie on her toast. "The days when we used to actually write letters."

"You did?" Sara asked. "So you've been writing for a long time. Are you still in touch with her? Did you get to see her while you're visiting?"

Ken once again leaned over and touched his wife's hand. "Sara, remember…"

Sara gulped and looked sheepishly at Rachel who only shrugged her shoulders. "Really, it's okay. Sara just thought she would ask all the questions at once." She turned to Sara and gave the express version of her relationship with Jenny and how Jenny had quite writing.

"That's so sad," Sara sighed. "But that could be your next book!"

Rachel was swallowing her brie-filled toast and coughed. Why hadn't that occurred to her? "Maybe," she said. "Or the one after the next one."

"Just as long you as you don't quit writing," Sara warned. "You can't stop writing. We won't have anything to read or discuss over tea if we don't have your stories."

Rachel smiled. She knew there would be days when she would wish to hear Sara say that over and over. It would have been nice to have it recorded so she could play it each time she needed to hear it.

*****

When they returned to Coolum, it was as if they hadn't left.

"That was like a trip within a trip," Rachel said, taking her bag up to her condo.

"Next time you come, we'll have to go to Fraser Island," Jamie said, following her up the stairs.

Rachel stopped and turned around. "Next time?"

"Yes, next time." Jamie said it as if it wasn't open for discussion. Wasn't it? She wondered.

"But maybe I don't want to come back," she suggested, looking for her condo key.

He laughed and opened his door. "Right."

Chapter 12

Monday morning meant the start of Rachel's last week in Australia. A small part of her missed home. She missed the familiarity of her house, her routine, and her surroundings. Because it was the beginning of June, that meant it was time to plant flowers and wipe down the patio furniture.

She knew her friends missed her and their Friday burrito nights at her house. At the end of the semester, she did it for her advanced fiction-writing students as well.

What she found though was that she didn't miss as much about home as she envisioned she would.

Am I more adaptable than I thought I was? Rachel wondered as she took a morning walk on the beach. Learning to walk on the left hadn't proven to be that hard although she hadn't attempted to drive yet.

There was a little tourism stand in the center of town and Rachel stopped there to see if they had any information on the Phillips family. She knew it was a long shot since they had moved twenty years ago but surely someone remembered them. They had lived there almost twenty years as it was.

"That name doesn't sound familiar to me," the first woman said, calling the attention of the second woman who wasn't listening.

"Oh, yes, Lance Phillips was the head police officer," the second woman said. "You might want to try the police station. I know they moved to Brisbane but that was the last I heard of them."

Rachel thanked them and walked the two blocks to the small building that served as the police station. The size reminded her how safe the town was. They didn't need a huge police force, nor had she even seen one police officer or car since arriving in Coolum.

Inside, she felt a little strange making her request but then remembered what she had been saying: life brings us where we're supposed to be at any given time.

"Oh Gary McCallahan would know them," said the man in a uniform at the front desk. "But he's on vacation for a few more days. He'll be here on Thursday if you'd like to check back."

A break at last. She hoped Gary McCallahan could give her some help. Walking back to the resort, Rachel began to wonder if maybe they moved again. It didn't seem likely from what Jenny's letters had indicated. But it was possible since twenty years had gone by.

In the meantime, Rachel felt some relief. In fact a lot of relief. There was hope that she still might find Jenny Phillips before she went home. She wished now that maybe she had tried a little harder when she had arrived. Her focus had been on the conflict in the book. Once again, she was too involved in creating something that she forgot that she was supposed to live life.

But she stopped herself and her thinking. That wasn't really true. She had been living. She had spent a lot of time with Jamie and he'd immersed her into Australian life. Or maybe she'd been spending too much time with Jamie rather than searching for Jenny. That couldn't be right. That didn't make sense.

Life puts you where you're supposed to be, she thought again.

And as the thought trailed through her brain, she realized she was supposed to spend the time with Jamie. She sat down on a wooden bench that overlooked the ocean. Below her, the waves washed up on the rocks rather than the beach. She watched it and thought about how much Jamie had taught her. He'd been good for her. And she wondered if she had been good for him. They had been brought together for a short time to help each other.

It was kind of sad that it only would be for such a short time though. She couldn't wait to tell him about her break. She knocked on his door when she reached the resort but there was no answer. She thought he was on the beach surfing and left him a note to find her on the balcony when he got in.

While Rachel was waiting for Jamie to get back, she sat on her balcony for a while and listened to the ocean swells. Jenny had several boyfriends when they were writing and the relationships were much more serious than Rachel had experienced in the same time.

Rachel had brought some of Jenny's letters out with her onto the balcony. She picked up where she left off with the last one. She took herself back almost twenty years, right back into Coolum where she was now. It was a far cry from where she had read the letter when it first arrived. Rachel guessed it was either up in her room or at the kitchen table, waiting for her mom to serve dinner.

But now she was in Australia reflecting back on each letter. And this particular one explained how Jenny had lost her virginity poolside. At a boy named Mark's house. Jenny laughed now. She imagined what a big deal it had been for Jenny to reveal that to Rachel. She probably hadn't told any of her friends.

And here she was telling her pen friend who was an ocean away. At that time, Jenny was more than an ocean away, they were young and they could have been planets apart from each other. Neither one of them truly knew how far they were from each other except by looking at a globe.

Jenny was sixteen when it happened. Rachel remembered being slightly upset by it. Now that she was older, she realized it was because she hadn't been ready to travel down that road herself at that time. She couldn't believe she had a friend who did because most of her friends weren't ready either.

Jenny had made it sound like the greatest experience in the world. Looking back, Rachel now wondered if Jenny was the better writer than her. How could sex on a pool lounge chair, especially the first time, be so wonderful?

Rachel thought back to her several students in the fiction workshop who had written about first sexual encounters. Fictionalized, of course. None of them had been great. Some of them had been dubbed mistakes. Young women who allowed men to take them somewhere they were afraid to say no to. Rachel knew these girls were writing about it because they were trying to understand themselves and why they had given away something they would regret later.

Her own experience had been much later. She promised herself she would get through college first. She'd watched too many girls packing up their belongings in the dorm her freshman year at semester. "I'm pregnant," the girl would say as she threw her clothes into a suitcase. "We're going to get married."

They always looked like it was a death sentence. They knew deep inside that it wasn't the way to start a marriage. Or the way to begin young adulthood. But there were a few who really didn't want to go to college and thought this was their way out.

Rachel waited until she finished her bachelor's degree and entered graduate school. There was a freedom in having completed one degree. Maybe it was just the mere thought that she had finished one degree and it meant she could do anything she wanted. Degrees meant freedom to Rachel. But she knew from other people in her past that life events could change dreams.

Sitting outside, listening to the birds sing, Rachel wondered if Jenny got pregnant. Maybe that's why she stopped writing. Maybe she was embarrassed by it. They were seventeen when Jenny stopped writing. That would mean she had an almost 20-year-old son or daughter. It wasn't far fetched but it made Rachel sad if that was the case, that Jenny stopped writing because she was embarrassed by her situation.

Or maybe Rachel put out an air about sex during their teen years and Jenny was afraid to tell her she was pregnant. But Rachel didn't remember what she wrote now without having the luxury of seeing her letters.

The stories continue, Rachel thought, her mind conjuring up answers where she couldn't seem to find a break. She hoped now there was a break with Gary McCallahan.

She walked back inside to her laptop and started writing. No sense wasting the time, she thought. She could easily get in at least a few more pages before Jamie arrived. And she knew he could be back at any moment or in several hours.

*****

Rachel finished writing early and decided she could use the afternoon off. She grabbed the magazines she had bought at the store and took them to the pool with her. The sun was hot, by far the hottest day since she had arrived in Australia, and she slathered on the sunscreen when she heard a voice.

"Want some company?" Jamie grinned at her as he dropped his towel on the next lounge chair over.

"Sure, but I don't think you're giving me any choice," she joked, spraying her shoulders and back, the spots she always missed.

"Is anyone staying here?" she whispered to Jamie, looking around as she dropped the sunscreen back into her bag.

"That's the beauty of this time of year," Jamie reminded her. "Places like this that are full in the summer are pretty empty around now." He threw his arms out and added, "So you don't have to share."

"I didn't come here to get tan," she admitted. "But I imagine that in Sydney you have to share your waves any time of year?"

"Yeah, but I expect that at home. I know that when I escape up here, it's something different."

Jamie dove into the pool and came up wiping his hair off his face. While Rachel had seen him several times with a wet head, when his hair was slicked back off his face it made his features more pronounced.

She walked into the pool gingerly, as if there were seashells on the bottom that might cut her feet, and he came up close to her. The water was just shallow enough that they could sit in the shallow end, as they might in the ocean, and let the water lap over them. "You have some scars on your face," Rachel finally verbally noted. "Are those from surfing?"

Jamie laughed. "How did you know?" He felt for one near his ear though and tapped on it. "That one is from falling off my bike when I was six though."

Rachel grimaced, wondering what else he injured falling off his bike.

She was content to sit there in the pool and let the water clear her mind, her body, her entire self.

"I wanted to ask you something," Jamie said, skimming his palm on the water.

Rachel looked over and shoved her sunglasses on top of her head. She was glad for the shade of the canvas covering. She had no idea what was coming.

"Are you ever angry about what happened to you? That your husband died?"

Rachel let out a slight smile. She knew Jamie felt more comfortable asking about something other than her writing and Jenny now that they'd had that talk in Hervey Bay. It appeared that everything was open for discussion now. Well, almost everything. There were some things Rachel wasn't ready to tackle with him.

"I know there were times I was, mostly before he died. I think what bothered me was knowing that my life wasn't going to be what I thought it was going to be. That was hard to accept."

"In what way?"

"I always thought Tom and I would have some kids and do the family thing. We were just about at that point, where we were stable enough financially and career wise, when he got sick. We had talked about my going off the pill just a few months before but for some reason I had a few months left of my prescription so I was being cheap and thought I'd wait and use up the ones I had."

"Do you think that was stupid?" Jamie asked.

Rachel leaned back and shrugged her shoulders. "Hindsight is 20-20, you know. I could have gotten pregnant and had a child to raise without him yet still had part of him with me. Or it was the universe's way of saving me from having to raise a child without him who was part of him."

"How do you feel today?"

"It's probably better I didn't get pregnant. I see it more that I was saved from something that would have been really difficult for me. I'm not one of those people who wants to raise a child on my own."

But Rachel knew she made it sound more simple that it was. She remembered being in the grocery store a few weeks before her trip to Australia. She needed brown sugar which sent her down the baking aisle. There was another woman in the aisle and Rachel had been grateful the aisles at the large store were wide enough that they could slide their carts past each other.

When Rachel glanced up, she saw where the woman had stopped. Right in front of cake decorating items. In every grocery store she went to, Rachel knew there was a section in the baking aisle devoted to candles and the store-bought icing people could get to wish someone a happy birthday.

She knew this well because her mother used it for all their birthdays. Each time a new birthday rolled around, her mother checked her supply in that family member's favorite color. When they were younger, she sometimes would also buy some of the plastic animals that could be placed on top of the cake with the candles.

On this day, the woman appeared to be debating which color would be best with which candles. Rachel didn't know for sure but that was the story she made up in her mind. Rachel wondered who was at home, who was getting a cake? Was it that night?

As she placed the bag of brown sugar in her cart with her tortillas, cheese, orange juice, and eggs, she was reminded how she had hoped to have that kind of experience with Tom. While they had cakes for each other's birthdays and other events, like when Rachel reached tenure at the university, it wasn't the same as party planning for a child.

Rachel sighed and moved on. She still needed lettuce and fruit.

"Do you still want to have a child?" Jamie's hair had dried and he ducked back under water while Rachel watered herself with her hands. Even in the shade it was hot. The hotel manager had told her they were in a drought but this was the first day Rachel had felt it after all the rain they'd had recently, particularly in the evening hours. She had come to find a lot of comfort in the sound of drops of rain against the tin roof of her condo.

"Ah, perhaps you brought it from America," the manager had joked. "You need to stay so we can end our drought."

But while Rachel was sitting in the pool with Jamie, the conversation was serious. Jamie was asking her the same level of questions that she had asked him in Hervey Bay.

Intimate was the word that came to mind for her. Intimate but not sexual. Or was it sexual? She tried to file that thought in her brain for the manuscript later, for Melinda to contemplate. Her hands were too wet to write it down.

She kept looking over at her things though.

"Do you need to write something down?" Jamie finally asked.

Rachel laughed. "Is it that obvious?"

"You better go do it," he urged. "I'm not going anywhere. It's too hot to go anywhere. I just hope it's not about me."

Rachel laughed and climbed out of the pool. "Not this time," she joked. Grabbing her towel to wipe off her hands and arms to keep the paper dry, Rachel jotted her thoughts down and waded back into the pool.

"You haven't answered my question yet," he reminded her. "I hope that wasn't a distraction." He smiled and she knew he was teasing.

"No, I had a thought." She took a breath before she answered. "I don't know about the kid thing. We'll see. I don't know what life is going to bring."

"You mean like how you came to Australia to find your pen pal and sign books and you ended up spending a bunch of time with me?"

"Yes, sort of like that," she said.

"What was he like?"

"Who?" Rachel had a lapse. "You mean Tom?"

"Yeah, what was Tom like? You talk about him yet you don't really talk about what he was like."

Rachel wondered where to start. She looked up at the sky from the edge of the canvas covering over the pool as if the answers were there. "He was my best friend. He was an architect which meant he was creative but also meticulous. He was fun. He believed in me. And he was the handsomest bald man in the world."

Jamie laughed.

"We actually had a joke about that," she admitted. "I called him that all the time." She shook her head, remembering what a big deal it was when Tom asked her to kiss the top of his bald head and she had agreed to do it.

"That just sealed the deal," he had told Rachel. "No other woman has agreed to kiss my bald head."

"I doubt you've been bald all your life though," she reminded him, giggling as he got up from where he knelt on the floor so she could do it.

"I don't remember the bad things," Rachel told Jamie. "I don't know if it's because he's gone so I can't remember the bad things and I've elevated him to some sort of pedestal. Or if it's because there wasn't time for the bad stuff to really happen. We didn't even have enough time for the seven-year itch because he was dying in the midst of it."

"You know how strong you are?" Jamie asked. They caught each other's eyes at the same time.

She opened her mouth and nothing came out.

"You are. You've been through a lot. I probably would still be curled up in a ball in bed if I loved someone and she got sick and died like you've been through. But you've turned your tragedy into an incredible strength by writing novels."

Rachel laughed. "No, Jamie, you'd be out surfing. At some point, you'd want out of that bed. Or if you didn't get up, your friends would drag you out of it."

"But no one had to drag you out of it?"

She knew he was right. She felt the need to swim away from him.

"Where are you going?" he asked, coming after her into the deep end where she slipped underwater and let her dripping hair cool her off when she re-emerged. "You should be pretty comfortable with these compliments, right?" Jamie asked. He was treading water while she held onto the ledge.

Rachel folded her arms underneath her on the ledge and rested her chin on her arms. It was almost too hot for her skin to touch anything but water. She tried to think how she could sit comfortably in the deep end. It was her own doing that she had left the safety of the shallow end.

"I know," she said. "Somehow it's different coming from you though." She finally looked over at him.

"Is that good or bad?"

Rachel laughed and swam back to the middle of the pool where he was. "I'm guessing it's all good. It's been a long time though, you know."

They were interrupted by two men coming into the pool area. The first other people Rachel had seen at the resort. She actually wished she could tell them how grateful she was that they had appeared. Her stomach had flipped when Jamie talked about her strength. Rachel knew there was an end date in sight. She couldn't allow herself to go down this road.

She climbed out of the pool and made herself at home on the lounge chair on top of her warmed beach towel. It amazed her that she actually could feel cool even though the air was almost 90 degrees. Her towel smelled crisp from the sun. A natural smell. But shortly she knew she'd be hot again. Maybe it was time to go inside.

"How about fish and chips for dinner?" Jamie asked, changing the subject and acting as if it was typical that they would spend dinner together. He assumed. Rachel smiled on both counts. She was glad he changed the subject.

Up in her condo, Rachel jumped in the shower, letting her wet bikini fall to the floor of the bathroom. As she let the warm water wash over her, she thought about how she let Jamie in. He had gotten further than anyone since Tom. But there wasn't anyone she wanted to be with until now. She hadn't thought that was bad.

Rachel hoped that time would bring her a man when it was supposed to happen. But why in Australia? Was she being tested to show herself that she was ready?

She washed her hair and wrapped herself in two towels, one around her head like a turban, and another around her body and walked back into the bedroom where she lay down on the bed for a few minutes.

A bolt of lightning hit and jolted her from her thoughts. The heat had caused a disturbance over the ocean and it was rolling in now. She hadn't paid much attention to it since it was very hot by the pool. And sunny.

Rachel got up and combed her wet hair. She could work on Melinda's contemplation of what kind of conversation could be considered intimate in the few hours she had until they would go to dinner.

It was still pouring when she met Jamie at their front doors. "I don't have an umbrella," he said. "But they do at the front desk. I'll run over there and get it and come back and get you."

Rachel looked at him, then down at her short denim shorts and black tank top. "I won't melt," she said.

"But you'll get wet," he said.

"Whatever," she added, shrugging him off. "I'm going with you. No reason to come back."

And off they went running past the pool to the reception area where Jason had the umbrella on the counter waiting.

Even in the rain, they walked along the beach. The thunder and lightning had let up and now the rain fell steadily.

There was an area of flat black rocks near the beach that led to the main town area of Coolum. Rachel pointed them out as they walked by and the ocean's edge lapped up against them, sometimes causing the water to rise up like it was spitting. Other times, not quite getting close enough to the rocks to do anything but roll back.

"They look so shiny when they're wet, like they are now," she said. "I mean, any rock or shell that the water hits is shiny when it's wet. But it's deceiving because they don't shine when they dry out. It's almost like in reality, nothing shines."

Jamie stopped and Rachel had to stop with him because he was holding the umbrella. "Where did that come from and what did it mean?" he asked. He smiled broadly but she could tell she had confused him.

Rachel tried to explain and then stopped herself. "I'm not really sure. That was pretty random, wasn't it?" she realized. "It made sense in my head."

He put his hand on her back and led her back toward town. She thought it was comfortable. She admitted to herself she liked it. But she was still thinking about the difference between the wet and dry rocks.

"You know," she said, hoping she had her thoughts better together, "life is random. From day to day we don't know what will happen."

"That's a good thing or we'd all be bored," Jamie pointed out, leading her up the boat ramp to the main road.

"I think one of my jobs as a writer is to connect people and that randomness. Almost like it's my job to help people help it make sense."

"Okay, at least that's a thought I can follow," Jamie teased her. He pointed toward the restaurant.

"This is what we'd call a dive in America," she whispered, leaning over to him when he opened the door.

"Are you insulting my restaurant?" Jamie asked, shaking out the umbrella before bringing it in the door.

"No," she whispered again, not wanting any of the restaurant people to hear what she said, "it's a good thing because these are the best kinds of places to eat." She gave him the "thumbs up" and he shook his head.

"You are way too random," Jamie joked as they slipped into a red booth by the window. He handed her a menu and she opened the laminated paper. "Let me not be so random now that we've arrived and tell you that I was planning to make you fish and chips."

Rachel's mouth fell open. "You were going to make them? Why didn't you?"

Jamie shook his head. "I don't think I could have pulled off anything edible in the kitchen at the resort. Next time you come, I'll have fish and chips for you."

Rachel looked at him and didn't say anything. Why did he continually think there would be a next time? He seemed to keep forgetting they lived in opposite hemispheres.

When the waitress had taken their orders and delivered their drinks, Rachel played with her napkin.

"Are you tired from sitting in the sun today?" he asked, putting his drink down.

"A little," she admitted, feeling a yawn come on now that he mentioned the word tired. When she looked in the mirror after getting out of the shower, she saw that she had gotten a little sun. At least when she went home, no one would think she only wrote and didn't emerge from the condo the whole time she was there. But she had also written several pages. And some of the discussions with Jamie were a little emotional.

"We were talking about death earlier today," she reminded him, staring at his Billabong t-shirt.

"Tom's death," Jamie added.

"And I was thinking about how you asked about me talking about him. When he died, there was so much paperwork to close out his life. It was awful. I had to take care of anything that had his name on it and people don't realize how much work that is. From social security to credit cards to his airline frequent flyer miles, I had to go through all his things and make sure it all was taken care of."

"It's a lot of work to end a life that's gone," Jamie added.

"Exactly. I couldn't do it all in one day either. And it would be a year later and I'd remember something I hadn't taken care of or something would come in the mail to him. Heck, he's still getting mail all these years later."

Rachel believed that he still got mail to remind her that he wasn't gone from her life. He never would be. He was still part of her past. And she still believed he was leading her although she also realized that was changing. Yet she still couldn't quite put her finger on how it was being altered.

Their food arrived and Rachel tapped her fingers on the table, anxious to dive into her meal. "Mmmm," she said, admiring what looked like perfectly cooked french fries. "Is there some ketchup for the fries?" she asked, looking around the table.

"Fries?" Jamie asked. He looked slightly confused.

"These?" Rachel pointed at the basket next to her meat pie.

"Oh, chips," he said.

"Fries," she said. "Chips are much thinner and crispier. And come in bags in the snack section at the store."

"Fish and chips," he reminded her, finally getting up to retrieve ketchup packets.

Rachel savored her meal and enjoyed Jamie's company, but when they got back to the resort, she was glad to return to her room alone. She had felt considerably more tired as the evening went on. It was the most she had talked and thought about Tom in a long time. All her fleeting thoughts throughout the days and nights added together were nothing compared to that day at the pool. But she also realized it might have to do with Jamie's comment about her strength. It was intimate. They were getting intimate with their sharing. And it only was a matter of time before it reached another level. One they didn't have time for.

"You look tired," Jamie said when they were back up the stairs in front of their doors again. The rain had stopped but he was still holding the umbrella in his hand. He'd return it to the front desk in the morning.

"A lot of stuff in one day," Rachel admitted. "Work, play…" She leaned against the wall between the doors to prop herself up. "Thanks for taking me to dinner," she told him.

"Any time." He came close and she shut her eyes, feeling his lips on her forehead. When she opened them, he was pulling back. "Get some sleep," he whispered, squeezing her hand. "I don't want to be accused of keeping the writer from getting her manuscript finished. You need to work tomorrow."

"And you need to surf," she reminded him.

Rachel barely made it into bed. She knew she was also sleepy because it was almost 10:00 pm and that meant she was way past her Australian bed time. She was glad Jamie at least hadn't made fun of her for that.

She drifted off quickly and slept soundly for almost seven hours. When she woke up, something about Tom stirred her. She wasn't sure what it was. She'd been dreaming life was as it was before. Years ago. When Rachel was awake

95

enough to realize what was going on, she didn't understand why she was thinking about Tom this much.

Why did she have the sense that Tom was pushing her away but something was still keeping them connected? The only sense she could make of it was that this was the conclusion. Or the conclusion was coming. It had been years since thoughts of Tom kept her up at night. Something was going on, something she still didn't understand.

It was time for a call home. She dialed Tanya's cell phone number but it was off. Rachel calculated the time and realized Tanya was probably at the pool with her daughters. She had caught the weather map of the US somewhere and it looked like it was hot in Kansas.

"I can't figure this out on my own," she said out loud grabbing Charlie and the rosary. "Please help me to understand what's going on, Tom. God. Universe. Whoever is listening."

When she rolled back over, she thought about her friends and their kids. How different were the roads they traveled. The group of them had initially become friends before they all were married. Tanya was Rachel's oldest friend in Kansas. They went to graduate school together although Tanya had finished with her master's and taught high school English. Chris had been a neighbor to Tanya and Stephanie was friends with Chris. Karen was the newcomer to the group, being Rachel's neighbor in her current house although it wasn't until after Tom died that their friendship emerged past neighborliness. She was the Martha Stewart Jr. in the group, showing up with muffins the day Rachel and Tom moved in. In a basket, no less.

All of them still had their husbands although it looked like Stephanie's marriage would end sooner than later. She had an inkling he had found someone else and she had been mustering up the strength to confront him about it. Rachel knew that by the time she got home, life could have radically changed for Stephanie.

Throughout everything, these women had been her confidants, even before she had an agent and an editor who saw her writing career through. But something kept her from telling them what was going on in Australia. She had the feeling she was supposed to work it out for herself before going to them and sharing with them all that had happened.

What Rachel loved best about her friends was that she never felt left out just because she didn't have a husband now. She often joked they were one big family.

"And you're the matriarch of us all," Chris had joked as she got up for another piece of cake the evening Rachel had said it.

"No way," Rachel said. "I am not the fearless leader."

"Yes, you are," the others chimed in.

"You are the pillar here. The matriarch always loses her husband and she's forced to go forward on her own," Karen said.

"That's stupid," Rachel. "Who wrote that crap? The matriarch should be happily married with a tribe of kids. That's the sign of a true leader."

"Not in your first book," Stephanie laughed.

Rachel knew she wasn't getting out of this one. She'd earned a new title and some day they would show up with a tiara for her. Really, she didn't care. No matter what happened, Rachel knew she could rely on them to be there for her and be a part of all facets of her life.

She must've drifted off to sleep because when she woke up, it was an hour later and she realized she needed to get up and get the day started.

"The manuscript won't happen if I don't write it," she mumbled, setting Charlie next to her laptop with the rosary.

Chapter 13

On Thursday, she walked back into town and made her way to the police station. The officer remembered her and immediately went to find Gary McCallahan. He was an older man and Rachel guessed he was Jenny's dad's age.

"Oh yes, of course I remember Lance Phillips," he said in a jolly voice with bright pink cheeks. "Good man. Good family. They moved to Brisbane."

"Have you heard anything from them?" she asked him.

He thought for a moment, scratched his head. "It's been a long time. I know I have their address around here though." He went back to his office and returned with a piece of paper.

When Rachel saw it, she wasn't sure if her heart should fall or pump faster. It was the same address she had.

"I can't remember the last time I heard from him but that's probably still a current address. We have him on a list here because he worked here almost twenty years."

Rachel thanked him and trekked back to the resort. This had to be a good thing, she told herself. This meant that the address she had was still current. If they still lived there, then why had Jenny stopped writing?

Rachel didn't want to say anything to Jamie but she was getting used to spending a lot of time with him. She felt a little like she was back in college and he was living in the dorm room next to hers; or like during graduate school, in the apartment across the hall.

While it had been partly sunny when she woke up early in the morning, she could see some clouds and hoped they would burn off and create another warm, sunny day. It turned into just the opposite though. As Rachel sat typing on the balcony, she heard the pitter patter of rain on the tin roof above her. She started to pull the table, her laptop sitting on it, toward the sliding doors when Jamie popped his head out. The storm from the night before wasn't quite finished.

"G'day," he said, his hair wet, leaning his surfboard on the side.

"Hi," Rachel said feeling like the computer was safe and she could sit again.

"They said it's supposed to rain all day. Are you going to write all day?"

"Not if I can get a few more pages done."

"Then I'll pick you up around 4:00 for dinner in town," he suggested.

"Okay," Rachel laughed, picturing him walking to her door and knocking on it rather than her listening for him to walk outside where she would meet him by the outdoor steps.

When he was gone, she reread the sentence she hadn't finished and sat back for a moment and watched the rain fall through the trees in front of her. This has to come together, she thought, hoping she could get in about ten pages before Jamie knocked on her door. She set back to typing and heard her cell phone ring inside the condo.

"Hello Rachel, it's Marian."

"Hi, Marian," Rachel said, almost relieved that the phone had rung and taken her away from the writing. She could feel herself inviting the distraction. That wasn't a good thing if she was going to complete a rough draft before going home.

"Listen, since you're staying in Australia a few more days, I talked to the people at Bartlow's Bookstore in Brisbane," she had to slow down to say the mouthful, "and they'd love to have you for a signing before you go home."

Rachel's mouth opened. "But this is my vacation. Or at least it's supposed to be." She glanced at the open laptop now sitting on the counter. Then she remembered Brisbane was the last address of Jenny's family. Maybe there was still hope.

"I can change your plane ticket and pay the extra hotel if you want to stay," Marian said. "That won't be an issue. I don't know why they didn't schedule you before but they called several days ago because they sold out of your books after the tv appearance. I was out of the office and just got the message."

"Book it and email me the info."

She worked through the afternoon on the balcony, listening to the rain tap against the roof and hit the trees outside the balcony. When she saw the lightning out of the corner of her eye, she moved to the counter where Charlie kept her company.

This is good, Rachel thought, taking down some of the self-stick notes she'd stuck to the wall with thoughts. The pile finally was shrinking rather than getting bigger. She couldn't stop thinking about Jenny though. Maybe she would come to the book signing. It could happen.

Jamie had his hand on the door to knock when she threw it open. "Aha!" she laughed, impressed that she could time how quickly he could get out his door and to hers.

"You have heaps of tricks, don't you?" he laughed following her down the stairs. They removed their shoes where the sand path started at the parking area by the beach. The rain finally had let up although it was still cloudy.

"I got asked to do a signing in Brisbane," she told Jamie, walking closer to the water than him. She jumped when it swelled over her feet and looked like it might not stop.

"Really?" he asked. "When?"

Rachel shared the details and explained how it came about. "I wasn't going to turn it down. There's still a chance I could find Jenny."

"Good on you," he said. "And to think I've been spending all this time with a famous person. Maybe I could write a tell-all book about these last few weeks when it's over and be able to quit my estate agent job. I could surf all day just because I befriended you."

"You thought I was just cute sitting there on my balcony with my laptop."

"Actually, you're right," he said. "And I wanted to make sure I spent my vacation with a cute woman." He paused. "You know, I flew into Brisbane. And my flight leaves the day after your book signing. How about if we go together?"

"You want to go to my book signing?" she asked, slightly surprised.

"I want to see what the fuss is all about. And I feel like I know Jenny," he said, half joking. "If she shows up, I want to meet her for myself."

Rachel couldn't believe what she was hearing. Another day together. Another trip together. If it had an ending point, why not give it another day?

They inched toward the center of Coolum, the few towering condo and hotel buildings growing larger as they got closer.

She looked over at him, walking easily down the beach as if he was one with it. And she knew he felt that way. Each morning he was out in the surf, looking for that perfect wave. Just the same as she was up searching for the perfect words to describe what she wanted to convey in the manuscript.

Everyone had to have a passion, she knew. Without one, who are we anyway? She wondered.

"Where are we eating tonight?" she asked, following him up the boat ramp.

"I thought it was time you had some kangaroo."

"Do you eat kangaroo?" she asked, not having heard much about eating it.

"Only when people come to visit from America," he teased opening the door to a small upscale restaurant in the center of town.

"That means never then," Rachel figured out verbally. "After I have kangaroo, will I have had everything I need to experience in Australia?"

Jamie thought for a moment. "You haven't surfed yet," he realized.

"And I'm not going to," she said, holding out a hand in front of her to stop his thoughts. "I think I've done enough for one trip. We'll leave it at kangaroo."

"Next time," he said.

"You think there will be a next time," she sighed, opening her menu so he couldn't see her.

"There will be," Jamie said, opening his own menu. They sat at the table in their own separate worlds, if just for a few minutes, while they decided what to order.

"The kangaroo wasn't bad," Rachel told Jamie on the walk back to the resort after dinner. The sun had come back out and was setting into the horizon. In a matter of an hour, the ocean and the sky would blend into one for the night. Rachel wondered if it had to do that before the sun could come up again in the morning. They had to come together to separate for a new day.

Rachel stopped. "Can we sit for awhile?" she asked Jamie. He plopped himself on the sand before she could do the same. "Was there ever a time you didn't love the ocean?" she asked him.

He shook his head and ran his hand through his hair. "No, I was in the ocean before I can remember it. I only know it because of the photos I have of my parents holding me up and letting the waves crash over me."

"So they were preparing you to surf?"

Jamie smiled at Rachel. "Little did they know what a mistake they were making." He was quiet for a moment; they both watched the water swing back and forth in front of them. "It's the same for you. Was there ever a time you didn't want to be a writer?"

"There was," she admitted, giving him the same smile.

"Really? That surprises me." He dug his feet into the sand.

"I know I told you that it started in high school but it got derailed in college." Talking about Tom wasn't painful for Rachel, talking about her early fiction career was. "I don't know why but I wrote the weakest female characters in the world."

Jamie fell backward with laughter. "That I don't believe!"

"Yes!" Rachel cried. "It's true!"

"I just can't believe that."

"Really! I had this fiction writing class. It was just like the workshop class that I teach now which makes it really interesting because my students have no idea how bad of a writer I ultimately was.

"There were about fifteen of us and we had a project that we would be working on and that we'd have to share with the rest of the class. I was really into country music at the time and thought it would be cool to live out on a ranch."

Jamie started to laugh again. Rachel tapped his knee lightly with her fingers. "Stop it and let me finish or I'll start having fits of laughter myself." She swallowed and started up again. "So this woman's name was Trisha, like Trisha Yearwood the country singer who was hitting it big at the time, and she falls in love with a rancher guy. But she's a suburban girl. Still, it's a very romanticized ranch. Trisha doesn't have to get up at the crack of dawn, they live in a nice house. You get the picture."

Rachel kept talking but she realized it sounded more absurd by the moment. And embarrassing. "I don't even remember what exactly happened at the climax of the story but he rescues her from something."

"And that's why you didn't go the writing route at first?" Jamie asked, taking a deep breath to keep himself from laughing.

"Yeah," Rachel said, making half a smile. "It's really embarrassing. I don't ever tell my students now. I just tell them my writing has come a long way. I don't believe that we have to reveal everything about ourselves."

"Yet you do in your writing," he reminded her. "At least that's the way it sounds to me."

Rachel knew he was right. "But most people don't know that. They think I made it up. If they don't know me, they don't truly know how much of Rachel Monroe they are reading about. That's the beauty of being a writer."

They were quiet for a few moments, both watching the ocean lull their thoughts along. "You mentioned the climax. Do you really think about that stuff when you're writing?" he asked.

"To some extent. I think about themes, too. But I'm thinking about it more in the way of figuring out what I want to convey to the reader. What do I want them to walk away with? I don't wonder what the book club should be discussing. That is, even if they get past the wine to discuss the book."

Then there was the manuscript she had sent Jenny. The one that never got a response.

When Rachel had confided to Jenny that she wanted to be a writer, she had already started collecting thoughts in a notebook, ideas for a novel. Her parents had bought a computer but Rachel still found it easier to carry around a regular-sized notebook at the time. Although the wire would be smashed and the cover edges tear and wear away, the notebook was almost a badge of courage for her. Those were her thoughts, her ideas, and some day she planned to share them with the world.

"Well, don't sit on that book!" Jenny had written, "Get it out from under your bed and get it done! No one will read it if you don't finish it!"

Rachel took Jenny's words to heart. She meant get it done. Jenny didn't think anyone should waste time. Not too many people knew what Rachel was working on though. She didn't want people to know, especially until she finished it. And when she did finish it, Jenny would be the first person she would share it with.

However, it was the first of the letters that she sent to Jenny that went unanswered. And this she shared with Jamie on that night they sat on the beach, the sun having gone down and darkness settling quickly over them.

"I thought it was another reason she stopped writing me," she admitted. "Maybe my story was terrible. And then when I wrote those awful stories in college, I figured that those were messages that I wasn't supposed to be a writer. Instead I was supposed to teach writing."

She tried to hold the tears back but something about admitting this was freeing her. She let a piece of the past go. Maybe it was because she finally had reached a place she thought she would be a long time ago. But when that dream had died, suddenly it was a bonus that it really had come true. Rachel didn't know if Jamie could fully appreciate what she was telling him. It didn't matter. This wasn't really about Jamie anyway, she realized. It was about her and her journey.

"You are a lucky girl," Jamie said. "You've led an amazing life and you still have a long way to go. Not everyone can tell stories but obviously you can. I'm glad I've been able to spend this time with you."

"You don't know how many book club people would be jealous of the time you've had with me," she teased, trying to make light of what he had just said. "And you're a guy so you're not exactly my typical fan."

"I haven't even read any of your books but I think I'm your biggest fan."

He got up and extended his hand to Rachel to help her off the beach. They shook the sand from their clothes and wandered back up the dune and through the woodsy walk to the resort.

Rachel glanced up at Jamie when they were in the woods and silently said a prayer.

No matter what happens, God, thank you. Thank you for bringing Jamie to me. I've learned more about myself in these few weeks than I think I have in my thirty-eight years. I don't think it would have happened without him.

She really thought the story ended there. What else was there? They had two more nights in Coolum and then they were on to Brisbane. While she held out hope that she would still get back in touch with Jenny, there was peace coming over Rachel when she slipped between her sheets that night. Like the story had ended and she was in the resolution. The conflict was the realization that this was her journey about where she had come from to where she was now. She had changed. It wasn't about Jamie. He was simply a catalyst for it to happen.

Her dream that night confirmed it, too. Rachel dreamt that she had gone for a walk on the beach and when she returned, she had no shoes. When she woke up, she realized that not having any shoes meant she had changed. She couldn't go back and get the shoes. It wouldn't be the same.

And it was exactly how she felt.

Chapter 14

"I'm going to take you to the surf club for dinner," Jamie said, pointing toward the large windows that overlooked the ocean, "since it's our last night here."

"I thought we were going out for meat pies again?" she asked, feeling a little confused. She had been looking forward to another meat pie. "Do they have meat pies at the surf club?"

They had stopped and stood together on the shoreline. She loved the peace she sensed from the water in this part of the world. Despite the storm, despite the looming clouds overhead, it didn't feel threatening. It was comforting and made her almost want to curl up on the beach with a book. A cloudy, rainy day at home did that to her. Why should it be any different here?

"We'll do meat pies another day, I want to do this tonight," Jamie said. As if there would be another day.

As they walked up the boat ramp, he explained that the surf club benefitted the lifeguards who patrolled the beaches for free. There was a lot of history to them in Australia as she would see when they entered the building. But first, they stopped at the top of the ramp and looked over the ocean that now lurked below them.

"It's always important to remember how small we are in the scheme of things," Rachel pointed out. She pulled her blonde hair back with a hair tie, realizing she should have done it before they even left for the beach. Now it was messy and everywhere. She leaned on the railing to balance herself.

"It's just the ocean," a voice came from the other side of Jamie.

Rachel hadn't noticed anyone beside them and now saw a teenage boy standing there watching the ocean with them.

"You think you could outrun it?" Jamie asked him, slightly amused.

The boy shrugged his shoulders. "I'm just tired of it. Same old thing each day. It doesn't change, you know."

Rachel simply listened. Jamie had kids although his weren't of what she called the "questioning" age yet. They were still happy to be around their parents, even though they weren't together. Dad was still cool.

"What would make it better?" Jamie asked the boy. Rachel sensed he was really giving this boy a chance to speak and be heard. She hoped the boy would take it seriously.

He shrugged again. "I don't know, I wish we had more group activities. Seems like other places people do more fun stuff."

Rachel bit her lip. She thought about Jenny. Rachel remembered how she and Jenny were each envious of where the other lived. There was Rachel in the middle of Michigan. But to Jenny, it was the US that was exciting in itself. And for Rachel, Jenny lived in Australia, the country she so badly wanted to visit. Each had something the other thought was better. Each had something the other wanted.

Here she was in Australia now without Jenny and not getting the chance to share with her pen friend all Jenny had shared with her.

Jamie and the boy were still talking, now about surfing. No matter where Jamie was in Australia, he seemed to be near a beach or kept his surfboard in his car. At least that was the way it sounded to Rachel.

Jamie told the teen they needed to leave and guided Rachel toward the front doors of the surf club where they had to sign in.

"You know, I was thinking while you were talking," she said, "Jenny and I used to go back and forth about who lived in the better place. I always said she did because she lived near the ocean but to her, I lived in the United States, which was like the entertainment capital. I guess we don't appreciate what we have. You don't know what I would have given to have been raised on the beach. And that boy is bored with the beach."

"Then you might surf, too," Jamie said.

Rachel knew he was still convinced he'd get her up on a surfboard yet. She just laughed and let him lead her up the stairs.

After they had ordered and were sitting at their table that overlooked the ocean, she turned the beer in her hand around as if it might look different from another circular angle. "I keep thinking how Jenny is the reason I'm here. Yet she's not here with me."

Rachel looked out on the ocean. It was getting dark quickly, urged on by the cloudy skies. She could still see the white caps, making their way to the beach, then disappearing into the sand. No matter what happened in life, the ocean was always constant.

"And you know, the ocean never changes. I can go away from here for years and come back and it'll still be washing up on the beach," she said, amazed.

"Maybe Jenny is here with you," Jamie said, taking a drink of his own beer.

"You mean like she's died?" She still didn't want to think about Jenny dead. That couldn't be.

"I don't know," he said. "When that many miles separate people and in the years before we had email, you never know. I'm still surprised you haven't found her on Google. Or any of her family members."

And no one in Coolum seemed to know what had happened to the Phillips family once they moved to Brisbane. Something didn't add up for Rachel. She continued to look outside and then back at Jamie. "You know, it's almost like I'm not supposed to find her. I mean, there's got to be a reason why it's this difficult, you know?"

Their food arrived and Rachel changed the topic. She wanted to know more about the surf club, about the photographic history that lined the bar they sat near. And once again, Jamie told her how important the ocean was to the people who lived near it.

An addiction, Rachel thought as they walked back to the resort along the beach. It's almost like an addiction.

"Do you want to sit in the spa for awhile?" Jamie asked.

While Rachel felt a little alone with her thoughts, she tried to remember that her time with Jamie was almost over. The manuscript would get done on its own time. And there still was that long flight home where she could work. But why was she jumping ahead? They only had two more nights together after this one.

He was there when she arrived, slipping into the warmed water. The resort was still quiet and Rachel still wasn't complaining. "I hope I get to come back here one day," she said, looking up at the stars that had begun to shine across the sky. "It's one of the most peaceful places I've been."

"Maybe you should come back to Australia next fall, "Jamie suggested. "I'll be here."

Rachel laughed and realized after she did it that she hadn't meant it to come out like that. It made it sound like she thought it was a crazy idea. And it wasn't. It just didn't seem feasible for her to come to Australia every year after school let out.

Maybe she just didn't want Jamie to know that she was becoming...the only word that came to mind was, fond. She admitted that she was becoming fond of him. No, she was fond of him. She'd become fond of him that first day when he met her at the café for lunch and then cooked her dinner. Each day she liked him more and more.

But she hadn't allowed herself to let go. She couldn't. The ocean was too wide. So she laughed to keep it light. And it was just dark enough that she couldn't see his true expression. If Rachel hurt his feelings, he didn't show it. He just laughed along.

Besides, this was her journey. He was a catalyst and nothing more.

They didn't talk for what felt like longer than it was. Rachel had found on this trip that her sense of time had disappeared. After teaching classes and being on a schedule, once she reached Coolum, she put her watch with her jewelry and left it there in the little purple velvet bag. She knew she'd have to take it out for Brisbane but it had been nice not to think about time for a few weeks. She lived with the sun and where it was in the sky. That was enough for her.

"How come you aren't married now?" Jamie finally asked Rachel, catching her off guard as she tried to figure out how pruned her hands and feet were from sitting in the water.

"What?" she asked. "You know my husband died." She thought they had discussed all of this before.

"But you could easily be married now," Jamie said. He stared right at her and she felt her body shake. He was calling her out. "You're a pretty woman, you have a great career, what man wouldn't want to be with you?"

"I don't see them breaking my door down," she laughed nervously, looking around as if the fake rocks surrounding the hot tub might provide for better conversation.

"Do you act different at home?" Jamie readjusted his body in the tub. It wasn't the most comfortable seating arrangement. The water temperature, however, was perfect. Not too hot, not too cold.

She shrugged her shoulders and checked the back of her bikini top. Something told her to make sure it was still tied, as if she had been sending the wrong messages in Australia. "I don't think so."

"I just can't believe that you don't have a boyfriend. Surely, you're holding back something. You're an amazing woman."

She felt a little uncomfortable with what he was saying. This wasn't a road she wanted to enter, especially with two more days of seeing Jamie. How could they start something now? Would he drop her off at the airport and say, "Oh, see you next year." Rachel couldn't do that.

"Um, thank you," she said.

A bolt of lightning came across the sky from the ocean. Both of them launched out of the hot tub and grabbed their towels.

"You okay?" he asked. Rachel stood in her towel, letting the dryness warm her from the scare, the cool air, and from Jamie's compliments.

"Yeah," she said. She wrapped the towel around her as if she had gotten out of the shower and walked toward him. "I don't have the answers," she said. "I just know where I'm at in my life right now."

"And that's here with me," Jamie acknowledged.

"Yes," she said, afraid to let it go further. "But I'm getting on a plane in a few days and flying to the other side of a small lake where I don't even live on the coast like you do. I live in the middle of that mass called America."

"You know, Rachel, I'd have thought your husband's death would have taught you to grasp whatever life put in front of you. It must've taught you to enjoy what you have when you have it."

"It has," Rachel said, readjusting her towel. "And it also taught me that nothing lasts forever. And that's been the hardest lesson of all."

They walked quietly upstairs. She watched him put his key in the lock of his door. "Good night," she said.

He walked over to her and kissed her on the forehead to show he wasn't mad. She sighed, relieved. But also knowing that she had hurt him. "Good night. And I still say you're a beautiful woman, no matter where you live and where I live."

Rachel removed her bikini and slipped on her pajamas inside her condo. She grabbed Charlie and placed him next to her. "Since it's too early to call anyone at home, you're going to have to listen to me," she said to him. "I don't think I'm making a mistake. I know what reality is. And reality is that we live too far apart. Heck, I'm taking you far away from your home. Of course, I don't see you complaining."

She turned out the light and thought about going out to the balcony but she knew that Jamie probably would be there. Instead, she grabbed the rosary. She fingered the beads and made up some prayers of her own. First she talked to Tom. Then she asked him to help her find Jenny. And she asked him to help her figure out the conflict for the novel.

Something grabbed her. That was the conflict, wasn't it? She was right in the thick of it. She wasn't in the resolution like she thought. No, it was more than her journey. It was the manuscript as well. It began to feel like once she left Australia, it would come together. And it was like someone was saying, "Sit tight, you almost have it. Relax."

But surely that couldn't be why she and Jamie were brought together? Or maybe it was, so he could teach her something. And then it was time to move on. Didn't that happen all the time? Rachel thought back to high school and some of the relationships she had written Jenny about. They both had summer romances. The boys who came to visit relatives and friends and they spent the summer hanging out together at the pool, at the mall, at each other's houses. But in August everyone had to return home and back to school. It was sad but their time together came to a close and no one questioned it.

This was different. This couldn't be like that, Rachel thought. She reached up and let the back of her hand touch the wall behind her, the wall that connected her with Jamie. She wondered what he was thinking. And she hoped he wasn't upset. Rachel really felt it was better not to delve too deeply now because the pain would be that much worse when they parted in another two days. She was grateful they were going to Brisbane together; that definitely made travel a little easier. But she still had to be careful and not let her emotions run away.

He'll thank me later, she thought, drifting off to sleep.

Chapter 15

Rachel wasn't sure how she was going to get everything back into her bags. It had gotten easy to spread out in the condo since she was there for several weeks. She couldn't remember the last time she had been on a trip where she stayed in one place for that long. She and Tom had never vacationed more than a week because Tom had to be back at work if it was in the summer. And any other time of year, Rachel had a class to teach.

In her years alone, she had taken very few vacations. It was easier to stay home, especially because the publisher sent her away. Sometimes she would stay an extra day or two in places like London but she hadn't ever stayed in one spot for more than a week.

Putting the bag on the bed, her belongings spread around it like they had been on her bed at home before she left, she thought about how her perspective on many things had changed in just a few weeks. Rachel remembered her excitement before she left home. It was all about the unknown. The good unknown. What would Australia hold for her? Would she get to meet Jenny?

And now, each item she placed in the bag reminded her of the events that had unfolded in front of her just like a roll of carpet someone had let go. There were the book signings and the media appearances of course; the whole reason she had come to Australia. And there was the manuscript. She hadn't finished it although part of her understood a little of what was happening. She would get that chance when she got home. Gardening wouldn't take up all her time unless she let it. July was still free before she had to return to the university in August.

There was Jenny. She didn't get to find her although it wasn't quite over yet. Rachel knew there was still a possibility that she would get to find Jenny that next day after the book signing. Jenny might even show up at the signing. Although the timing had been short, Marian said that they were going to focus on the local book clubs to get people there. But the trip had also allowed her to understand more about her friend and her life. Rachel just wished she could share more with Jenny. She ached inside herself that somewhere out there Jenny was living her life while Rachel was traveling Jenny's country. Yet one didn't know where the other one was.

Finally, there was Jamie. Rachel hoped that time would give her a better reflection of what their relationship had been about. All Rachel could see as she packed was that Jamie had been brought to her to help her write and create the conflict for the manuscript. Life was messy and random. So were relationships. Melinda's life was no different in the manuscript.

"It can't be more than that," Rachel thought, wiping her hand on her forehead. She had almost everything in the bag. She hadn't bought that much so it had to fit. And Charlie was definitely riding in her carry-on bag just as he had after she bought him in the Melbourne Airport on the way to the Sunshine Coast.

She left the items she would need for the next two days near the top of the bag and thought about what she had expected from her trip, what she had been thinking about when she arrived at the Sunshine Coast airport, and how that had changed when she met Jamie.

Sometimes you have to experience life to have something to write about, she reminded herself. She told her students that often. She never told them they had to suffer to be writers. She didn't believe that. Although she knew people felt that way about her writing because it was Tom's death that propelled her career, she knew it wasn't true. Her writing was rooted in her teen years. She had taken a hiatus to live life.

It was because of Tom's death that she finally made it happen. She didn't have to suffer to be a writer. She just had to live life. And if she had to live life to experience the past three weeks to have a new manuscript ready for Marian by the end of the summer, well, then that was okay. She was going to have to accept that's the way it was supposed to be. Jamie had been her recent life experience.

Rachel set Charlie on top of her bag after she placed it back on the floor. She was done. She sat down on the bed and wondered what Jamie was doing next door. She didn't let her thoughts linger though. She couldn't. She grabbed the rosary and admired it for a few minutes and the importance of the beads.

We all need a little meditation sometimes, she thought, to ground us.

If she could achieve that with a set of beads, she knew she was doing well. And that thought sent her to sleep.

Chapter 16

"Whenever I come up here," Jamie said, packing their luggage into the back of the rental car late the next morning, "I always fly into Brisbane so that I can drive up the coast."

"I hate to leave," Rachel said, looking around at the resort where the sun had returned. "I'll be back home in three days."

"I guess we all have to return to reality," he joked. "Mine's waiting for me in Sydney, that's for sure."

Rachel climbed into the car beside him and took in more of Australia as they headed south along the coast. Because Brisbane was somewhat inland, Jamie turned off the coastal road and onto the motorway. The plan was to drive to Surfer's Paradise that night before flying to Sydney the next morning from Brisbane. Jamie assured her it was only a half hour drive between Surfer's and Brisbane and well worth the drive to spend a night on the beach if one had to stay somewhere.

When they arrived at the bookstore, Rachel didn't get out at first. "You know, ever since I got the call from Marian about the book signing, I've been hoping that maybe Jenny might show up. I mean she lived in Brisbane for awhile."

"I know," Jamie said, with a smile. "And if she doesn't, why don't we go and find the house after?"

"Are you serious?" Rachel's face lit up. "You'd do that for me?"

"I'll do you one better. While you're at the book signing, I'll go find out where the house is."

She put up her right hand in the air to high five him realizing that maybe she should have hugged him. No, she told herself, they were parting the next day.

"You're the best, you know that?"

Jamie smiled and grabbed her hand. "When you spend a lot of time with someone, you find you want to help them with more than telling them who serves the best meat pies in town."

While the book signing had been a quick schedule, Bartlow's hadn't wasted any time getting ready for Rachel and *Summer Bay*.

"I'll be back in about two hours," Jamie called as the bookstore owner Sandra tried to lead Rachel away from several women who wanted to talk to her. She nodded her head and waved.

It was two hours of non-stop talking and signing. Each time a woman came up to Rachel and acted excited to see her, Rachel hoped that person might be Jenny. Women in all shapes and sizes. All backgrounds. And some named Jenny. But no Jenny Phillips.

When Jamie appeared back at the bookstore, Rachel was swallowing water out of a water bottle. Her voice getting a little raspy from all the talking.

"That was wonderful," Sandra sighed. "We're so glad we were able to get you here. I can't even imagine what the crowd would have been if we'd planned this over a longer period of time."

"Maybe it's better you didn't," Jamie joked.

Sandra looked at Jamie and then back at Rachel. "Is this your boyfriend? I didn't know you had an Australian boyfriend?"

Rachel almost spit out her water right onto Sandra. Jamie beat her to the answer though. "No, I'm sure she has several of those back in the states," he said. "I'm just her Australian travel partner."

"Where did you come up with that?" she teased him as they walked back to the car. She didn't have time to think about it though. "Did you find out where the house is?"

Jamie handed her the directions written by a man at a gas station. "It should only take us about twenty minutes to get there."

"I'm a little nervous," Rachel admitted as Jamie pulled onto the motorway to take them to the suburbs.

"Ah, hopefully her parents live there and will tell you that she lives across the street with her husband and her two kids."

Her fingers crossed, Rachel hoped the same thing.

The house was brown, just as Jenny had described it. There were details that Rachel thought she could recite from memory: the addition in the back for her parents, the pool, the horses roaming on several acres. It was even better than Rachel's mind had imagined.

"Want me to go with you?" Jamie asked, pulling the car alongside the curb.

"Of course. I need you to hold me up from behind so I don't chicken out."

The driveway angled down off the high road to the house. She could see the horses roaming in the field behind it along with the fields and hills that appeared to sprawl forever. This was the paradise that Jenny wrote about in her last letters after they had moved from Coolum. A different paradise than the beach. And then the letters had stopped. Rachel hoped it was only because she was too busy enjoying her new life.

"What if they aren't happy that we showed up unannounced," Rachel whispered after she rang the doorbell. "You don't show up like this where I come from."

Jamie shook his head. "You do here."

She heard steps inside and the door opened, a woman with short grayish hair peered out. Rachel felt like she was back in Girl Scouts selling cookies to people she didn't know.

"Hi, are you Mrs. Phillips?"

"Yes," the woman said slowly and tentatively. She wasn't going budge opening the door more yet.

"I was Jenny's pen pal in America." It was obvious the woman was thinking, as if the wheels were turning. But instead of a smile, her face turned sad. "Rachel."

"Oh dear," she said.

Rachel wasn't sure what that meant.

"Who is it, love?" a voice called from behind.

Mrs. Phillips opened the door wider and Rachel could see a balding man strolling toward the front door. And he could see them.

"Who are they?" the man asked, looking Rachel and Jamie up and down.

"Lance, this is Rachel. She was Jenny's pen pal in America."

"Oh, dear," he also said. Looking at his wife, "You should invite them in for some tea."

Mrs. Phillips looked as if she needed direction. Rachel just wanted to know what was upsetting them. She felt Jamie's hand squeeze her shoulder and she was grateful for any strength he sent her way. She started to think all her happy fantasies about meeting back up with Jenny were about to be torn to shreds.

They were invited to the kitchen table and it was Mr. Phillips who began while Mrs. Phillips looked for some cookies and started the tea. "Well, I'm sure something brought you to Australia." He looked at Jamie as if Jamie was the reason.

"Oh no, he just drove me over here," Rachel said, looking at Jamie and realizing that it didn't come out right. She tapped her fingers on the white tablecloth for a moment. "I'm a writer," she said. "I was in Australia for some book signings and I did some television. I had a signing in Brisbane today. I go back to the US in two days."

"And what have you written?" Mrs. Phillips asked setting several cups on the table.

"*Summer Bay* is my most recent."

She looked surprised and then smiled, still standing next to the table. "I've seen it and I never made the connection."

When she finally sat down Mr. Phillips took a deep breath. "We knew we should have written and told you. But it was so difficult." He took another breath, leaning into the table. "Jenny was killed in a car accident a few miles away. That's why you stopped receiving letters from her."

Rachel gasped. Her fear had come true. Or was it relief? Her fear that Jenny died. Her relief that Jenny hadn't forgotten her. Underneath the table, she felt Jamie's hand take hers and hold it. He wouldn't let go until they got up to leave the table what seemed like hours later. She wanted to turn to him, to acknowledge all that she had shared with him. But that would have to wait. Mrs. Phillips began to speak.

"Your letters continued to come and we were so grief-stricken that we couldn't bear to answer them. And as more time went by, we, well, it became easier not to answer them." She used a napkin to wipe her eyes. "I hope you'll forgive us."

Rachel then relayed the story of how she thought Jenny had stopped writing because Rachel hadn't found any information on the actor from the television show "V."

"Oh gosh," Mrs. Phillips laughed. "He was quite the handsome man. Of course I don't remember his name now."

"I can't remember his name either," Rachel laughed. "And now it would be so much easier to find him with the Internet," Rachel reminded her.

"We're just so glad you came," Mrs. Phillips said, touching Rachel's hand.

"I'm sure you never expected me to end up at your door," Rachel said, half a smile on her face.

"We never ever expected to see you here," Mr. Phillips laughed.

"She so enjoyed writing you," Mrs. Phillips said. Rachel now could see that Jenny's death had made her older. She remembered the photos that Jenny had sent and her mom looked so youthful. While over twenty years had gone by, Rachel knew that she shouldn't look that old now. She guessed it had grayed her as well. "I remember when I'd find a letter or a package in the mail from you and set it out on the table here for when she got home from school."

Rachel could see it was a happy memory. Mr. Phillips got up and walked into the living room, coming back with photos of Jenny and her sisters.

Mr. Phillips promised to email her some more information about Jenny's death and photos of her, too. "I know you'll need time to process this, just as we did. Again, I'm really sorry we didn't allow you to do it twenty years ago."

Rachel could only nod her head by then. The lump in her throat continued to grow as they got closer to walking out the door.

By the time they left, Rachel was wiped out. Part of her still was in shock. But as they drove back toward Surfer's Paradise and the ocean, the tears began to fall.

"I'm sorry," Jamie said, "I know this wasn't what you imagined. It wasn't what I imagined either. I really wanted to see you reunited with your friend."

Rachel shook her head. "I just can't believe it." She was still shaking her head when they arrived at the hotel.

In the lobby of the hotel, Rachel walked with Jamie to the desk and explained there were two reservations for them. Rachel could barely focus, finding herself looking out the lobby windows and doors at the ocean across the street.

"What do you mean you only have one room?" Jamie asked, handing the woman his reservation that clearly showed he had requested two rooms.

"I'm sorry Mr. Stephens, we only have one room for you."

Rachel panicked. How could this day get any worse? How could they not have a room for each of them?

"Do you want the room or not?" The woman asked him acting like she was irritated with him for arguing with her even though he proved to her that he had booked two rooms. Jamie looked at Rachel.

"If I had to guess, you want to be alone tonight, but I can sleep on the balcony if that would help," he offered.

Rachel tried to smile. "No, it's okay. We'll work it out."

He turned back to the gum-smacking woman. "We'll take the room but make sure it has a great view of the South Pacific."

And it did. Rachel dropped her bags and walked straight out through the sliding glass doors that were already opened before they arrived. She sat down in one of the silver metal chairs and finally let go. It was as if someone had taken the hope away from her. For so many years, she believed she would make it to Australia to meet Jenny, even though Jenny had stopped writing, and now that was gone. It had been a focus off and on for parts of her life. She'd made it but Jenny was gone. Why did that happen?

Jamie came out and pulled the other chair next to her. She held her face in her hands. Her hair was matted against her face from the tears. She didn't care what he saw. They'd spent enough time together in the past few weeks. It didn't matter.

He rubbed her back and didn't say a word until Rachel felt the sobbing subside. At least for a while. She sat back up and finally acknowledged the blue and green water that sparkled out in front of her.

Jamie pushed the matted hair off her face. "I know you're tired and you probably want to climb into bed but I think we need to go get something to eat.

There's a great fish and chips place right on the beach just around the corner. My plan had been to take you there and I still want to."

Rachel nodded and got up to go splash cool water on her face. "Thank you," she said quietly, touching the top of his head as she went by.

She was embarrassed. She had no clue why she was this upset. It made no sense. She actually never knew Jenny. At least in person. But Jenny had been such a significant part of her life for her teen years. She was like a friend who moved away although they remained friends through letters. Only Jenny was in Australia and Jenny taught Rachel that life across the world was very similar.

They shared their dreams that were the same in many ways. While Jenny didn't want to be a writer, she wanted Rachel to share her writing with her. Jenny's dream had been to be a teacher, to use Rachel's writing in her high school classroom. And they both wanted boyfriends they loved and could rely on. And who were cute.

Jenny held the diary of Rachel's life just as Rachel now held the history of a life cut too short.

As Rachel wiped her face dry with a towel, she thought about how she at one time had everything both she and Jenny aspired for. She was teaching (although at a different level), she had written and published books. And she had a husband. While Tom had died, Rachel knew they always would have been together if he had lived. The cancer was beyond their control. Jenny was another loss, Rachel realized. Maybe that's what upset her.

She walked out of the bathroom and found Jamie opening his suitcase to change his shirt. As she watched him, not really focused on his stomach, his chest, or any other interesting part of his anatomy, she began to realize that their time together was near the end, like a battery that is in the red and about to run out of power. They both would return to their respective lives shortly.

Scratching her back, Rachel sat down on the bed. "I don't get why this is happening to me," she sighed.

"I do," Jamie said, slipping his feet back into his flip flops. "Conflict. Remember how you told me that you couldn't figure out the conflict?" She nodded, still not sure what he meant though. "You have your conflict now," he reminded her, folding his arms across his chest. "Sounds to me like loss is the conflict in your life. The theme."

Rachel tried not to gasp. What he said had crossed her mind in the last few days although not to this same extent. Her thoughts had been more about the journey and the catalyst for the journey. And yet there he spurted it out. It almost felt as if Jamie was reading her thoughts. No, he was reinforcing them. As he continued to talk, she felt her mouth drop open.

"I think you thought you could go through life without more conflict. Your husband was sick and died. You went on. You thought that was it."

"But you wanted me to find Jenny, too?"

"Of course I did," he said, sitting on the bed next to her. "Why would I want you to be anything but happy?"

As much as she fought it, Rachel knew he was right. Life wasn't neat. It wasn't pretty. It was a jagged line. And she had more conflict to come when they had to say goodbye.

They walked to Craig's Surf n Chips around the corner and ate at a table next to the sidewalk, facing the ocean. It was the middle of the week and there was only one other customer. As the sun set, just like north in Coolum, it cooled off. But Rachel would learn a little later that the noise in Surfer's Paradise didn't die with the sun. It went the other direction.

Walking on the beach, Jamie pulled her close to him and she didn't resist. Once again, she tried to pull all the strength she could from him. It felt like his poured over the top of his bucket and he had plenty to spare. And he was willing to share it with her. Jamie was part of this whether she liked it or not. He was sending her the strength that Tom once had sent her. It could only last for less than twenty-four hours though.

She allowed herself to let go. Rachel wondered at this point why she was holding back. Because they were going back to their own worlds the next day? Why was she allowing that to impede her feelings for Jamie? They'd been given this time for a reason. And maybe she'd wasted it.

By the time they reached the hotel again, Rachel was shivering. Even in the elevator she couldn't get warm. Jamie left the sliding glass doors cracked open, allowing them to hear the ocean noise, but she couldn't find warmth. He sat on the bed and reached for her. "Come here," he said, holding his arms out.

Nothing to lose, she told herself. It's okay. She didn't pull any strength now. She let herself rest.

She'd worked hard. No matter what she had tackled in life, she threw herself into it. Tom's illness, her doctorate, her teaching, her writing, appearances. Why had she thrown this time away with Jamie?

"I'm sorry," she whispered.

"Why?" He nudged her and pulled her up where he could see her face. "What are you sorry for?"

"I wasted our time," she admitted. "I now see how much you and I could have had over the last few weeks. I honestly was afraid to let myself have that much. Conflict." She laughed low.

Jamie smiled. "No, it was what it was supposed to be." He nudged her again and turned out the light next to him. The room was still bright from the street lights below. And noisy from the crowds walking by. There was no such thing as quiet in Surfer's Paradise.

"The later it gets, the noisier it will be," Jamie acknowledged. She felt his hand rubbing her back.

"Does that matter?" Rachel asked.

"Only if you're trying to sleep."

She felt him move his face closer to hers. It didn't matter now. Flying home was going to be painful no matter how she sliced it.

Chapter 17

When the sun came up, Rachel knew somewhere deep inside of her that being with Jamie had been what she was supposed to do. She pictured herself back at home over margaritas trying to explain this one to her friends. Surely they would laugh at her. No, she knew, they would be happy for her. She was the one adjusting to the idea of saying that she'd had a fling. And in Australia, no less. At least it sounded exotic. She pictured the reactions of her students if she announced it the first day back at class when she made them all tell her one exciting experience they had over the summer.

She pulled herself out of bed and looked into her bag for her glasses. She saw the rosary and realized she hadn't needed it or Charlie the night before. Rachel looked over at Jamie beginning to stir. She smiled at herself. He had given her that strength. Tom knew someone else was coming. Jamie had been the reason he'd been letting her go. If she clung to Tom, she wouldn't have been with Jamie.

The rosary had been temporary. Or maybe not, she thought, when she realized they would part ways later that morning. Maybe the rosary was permanent and Jamie was temporary.

It doesn't matter, she thought. The importance is that the strength is there.

As they took their final walk on the beach together, Rachel was lost in her thoughts. As long as Jamie didn't ask her for any, she didn't offer.

"You know, I've been thinking about Jenny and Tom since yesterday," she said and laughed a little. "I guess you aren't surprised by that."

Jamie squeezed her hand.

"When Jenny and I were writing, she had sex long before I did." Jamie looked at her a little confused and Rachel stopped her thought for a moment. "There's a reason I'm telling you this." She paused again. "I wasn't ready for that at the time. And I wasn't sure at the time how I felt about having a friend who had gone so much further than I had at fifteen." She stopped again and swallowed. "And she was also driving long before me. I mean, she didn't have her license and she had a boyfriend who would take her out. I didn't do that. I only went out with my parents until I got my license. She really lived life to its fullest."

"Do you think she knew something?"

Rachel nodded. "That's just it, I wonder if she did. I was always more tentative. And it was the same with Tom. He got out there and just did things. He didn't think twice. He didn't waste a moment. They were so much alike and they both died young. Yet it was like I somehow knew I'd have more time so I took that time. I don't know. It was just something I was thinking about."

They were quiet for a few minutes, each watching the tide roll out.

"Will it be hard for you?" she finally asked, changing the subject as if the pause in talking had been long enough to allow that.

"What?" He stopped to pick up an unusual shell.

"Will it be hard for you? After we part ways at the airport?"

"Oh," he shrugged his shoulders, "I have a stack of work probably up to my eyeballs at my desk. And then I need to have the house painted. And the car needs an oil change. Plus I have the kids this weekend. Nah, I'll be too busy."

He didn't look at her and Rachel's feelings took a turn. What was that supposed to mean?

Jamie stopped and wrapped his arms around her. "You are the silliest girl in the world, you know that?" He kissed her on the forehead. "Of course I'm going to miss you."

Rachel relaxed and rested her cheek on his sweatshirt.

"I'm only letting you go home because your world is there and you have a book to write," he said. "If you lived in Australia, I wouldn't let you go any-where without me."

That's what she needed to know.

Her cell phone rang and she wiped her tears away to see who it was. Since it was afternoon in the states, there was the feasibility that someone needed something from her. But she didn't recognize the number.

"Sounds like Brisbane," Jamie said, when she read it to him.

Rachel answered it. "Hello?"

"Hi Rachel, it's Mrs. Phillips," a calm voice said from the other end. "Jenny's mum."

"Oh, hi," Rachel said. "I didn't expect to hear from you."

"Well, we didn't expect to call you but we have something we wanted to give you. Is there any way you can come out to the house before your flight today?"

Rachel knew Jamie could hear what was going on and he nodded. "We can do it," he whispered.

It meant they had to leave earlier but Rachel was thankful that Jamie understood the importance although she was a little sad it meant less time alone together. Still, Jenny was Rachel's reason for everything Australia. Except the book sales.

Back at the front door of the Phillips' house, Rachel had no idea what they wanted to give her. Twenty years had gone by. What could they possibly still have of Jenny's now? Rachel knew how little existed of Tom's life now. It had been important in the beginning but now she didn't feel she needed to hold onto his life. She had two boxes labeled "Tom" near her childhood boxes and they were all she needed. The rest of him was with her.

"We're so glad you could make it," Mr. Phillips said, letting them into the house. "We know you can't stay long, but since Australia isn't around the corner from the US, we wanted to give you something."

Mrs. Phillips handed Rachel a stack of what looked like envelopes. Then Rachel saw it was all her letters to Jenny, many of them unopened. The letters she had sent not knowing that Jenny had died. And one big envelope. The manuscript that Jenny never read.

Rachel gulped and her eyes began to tear up. Her hands shook as she held them.

My diary, she thought. All right here in my hands now.

"We couldn't throw them away," Mrs. Phillips said. "I don't know what it was but something told us not to so we kept them in a box of Jenny's things all these years."

Rachel held them close to her and hugged both of them.

"We didn't mean to upset you before you went home but we really wanted you to have them."

Rachel couldn't even speak. She smiled and kept crying.

"And we hope you'll come back some day to spend some time with us," they said.

Rachel still couldn't speak but Jamie found her voice for her. "She'll be back sooner than she realizes," he said.

As they left, he wrapped his arm around her and she looked up at him and smiled. "The conflict is all right here," she said. "This is what I needed. Jenny made sure they held onto these because she knew the day would come when I would need them. I just didn't get it until now."

Jenny had been leading her life long before Tom had even entered it.

He kissed the top of her head and they drove to the airport.

*****

As the moment of goodbye ticked closer, Rachel tried to fake it. It was one of the few times where she needed Tanya. Or Chris. Or even Marian. All the people who had held her up in the times during her life and career when she needed them. Where were they now? Had they all been preparing her for this moment when she would need to do it on her own? She couldn't call any of them to fix it or give her the answers she needed.

Her plane was the first to leave. A fact she was grateful for. After arriving in Sydney, she'd need to collect her luggage and then recheck for the international flight. It felt like such a difficult task knowing how sad she was going to feel once Jamie walked away from her gate. Or as she walked through the jetway. Whichever came first.

In the car, before they returned the rental, she was gathering up her boarding pass and making sure she had her passport when he touched her and kissed her unexpectedly. "We can't do that in the airport you know," he said.

"Why not?" she asked.

"What if we don't realize it but we kiss next to the bookstore where your books are in a pile and someone recognizes you?"

126

"No one ever recognizes me," Rachel smiled. "That's the beauty of being a writer. No paparazzi."

"Okay, then we'll do this again by the bookstore in front of the books," he suggested.

Rachel hoped he wouldn't remember to do it though. She didn't want to take any chances of someone recognizing her on a day when she felt so sad.

"Look, Rachel, it's *Summer Bay*," he said a little loudly when they walked by the newsstand.

"Okay," she said wishing she could hide behind the magazine rack.

"Come on," he called, grabbing her arm and pulling her close to him. He caught her lips and kissed her hard. When Rachel pulled away she knew she couldn't do anything but smile. Jamie wasn't going to let her forget what a great time they'd had together.

Her hands shook when it was time to board the plane. She couldn't read her seat assignment. "I just didn't ever think that a trip like this could be so significant to my life," she admitted to him. They faced each other, their carry-on luggage at their sides as if they were walking their dogs and made them sit and wait while they chatted.

"That's the beauty of life," he said, "we don't even know what's in front of us. It's probably concealed for that reason."

Rachel nodded and focused on his University of New South Wales t-shirt.

This would be the last hug. The last kiss. The plane to Sydney, and the plane to San Francisco, weren't going to wait for her to not let go of a man. Planes still had schedules to keep. They didn't run on human feelings.

"You need to go," he whispered giving her a quick peck on her cheek and turning her toward the woman scanning the boarding slips.

It was then that Rachel realized this was going to be difficult for her. When she turned back he looked away quickly and waved his hand at her. She knew he didn't want her to see the emotion in his face.

Rachel didn't allow herself to look back at the gate area again after that because Jamie would be gone. He had to gather up his emotions before his own flight to Sydney. While they were going to the same place, they'd be on separate airlines and arriving at separate times. And Rachel knew she'd have no time to look for him at the airport there. She barely had enough time to collect her luggage and recheck through international. The trip home had begun.

Unlike her flight from Melbourne to the Sunshine Coast several weeks ago, this one was much more subdued. The party was over. Everyone was going back home. Back to work. Back to reality. And that included Rachel. She almost felt like everyone on the plane had something to mourn. Including her. It was selfish to think they were all mourning her life. No, they all had their own lives to live through.

Baggage. Recheck. More baggage. Security. Finally, she reached the gate area with forty-five minutes to wait. She browsed the shops but everything left her a little sad. She'd had companionship, Australian companionship for three weeks. Now she was alone again. But there still was a manuscript to finish when she got home.

Rachel realized the world wouldn't end that she came home with it unfinished. The reality was that Marian probably would tell her she was happy it wasn't completed.

"Sometimes you have to live a little life to have more to write about," Marian would say. In the past, Rachel might have snorted back at the comment when made about her own life, thinking about losing Tom, but not now. She had a different view. Jamie opened up a different world to her. She looked forward to getting onto the plane where she could at least relax for half a day and relish in the night before. And all he'd given her.

She pulled the book she wanted to read out of her bag and opened it to the page where she'd left off. That had been three weeks ago, before she and Jamie met as neighbors at the resort. There was no reading after that. Also in her bag were pages and pages of notes. And the scraps of paper from places they'd been where she'd made notes as things came to her that she hadn't added to the manuscript yet.

But before she could open the book, her cell phone buzzed. Who would be texting? She wondered. It was late in the states, about midnight.

"U kno Jenny brought us 2gethr," it said. "Ur life since u were young has been about coming to Aus. It was her job to bring u here so we could meet. U'll be back after you finish the book. I guarantee it."

Rachel smiled and held the phone next to her as if it was something treasured, not just a message. It was about who the message came from. And what it said. When she placed it back in her bag, she felt the rosary. Life had brought her comfort and hope in many ways.

She knew he was right. As the plane roared down the runway, heading back to the United States, Rachel could say to herself that she was going to be back. She watched the land give way to the ocean. He was right. Jenny had cleared the path. Once again, just like her career, loss had led the way to where she was supposed to be and what she was supposed to do. She opened the letters that comprised her diary and began to read, one by one.

www.ingramcontent.com/pod-product-compliance
Lightning Source LLC
Chambersburg PA
CBHW070752120626
46557CB00002B/562